Alternatives

Debating Theatre Culture in the Age of Con-Fusion

P.I.E.-Peter Lang

Bruxelles · Bern · Berlin · Frankfurt am Main · New York · Oxford · Wien

Dramaturgies

Texts, Cultures and Performances

Peter ECKERSALL, UCHINO Tadashi
& MORIYAMA Naoto (eds.)

Alternatives

Debating Theatre Culture in the Age of Con-Fusion

Dramaturgies
No.11

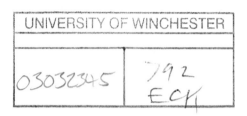

© P.I.E.-Peter Lang s.a.,

PRESSES INTERUNIVERSITAIRES EUROPÉENNES

Brussels, 2004

1 avenue Maurice, 1050 Brussels, Belgium

info@peterlang.com; www.peterlang.net

Printed in Germany

ISSN 1376-3199
ISBN 90-5201-175-3
US ISBN 0-8204-6621-2
D/2004/5678/15

*CIP available from the British Library, GB
and the Library of Congress, USA.*

Bibliographic information published by "Die Deutsche Bibliothek"

"Die Deutsche Bibliothek" lists this publication in the "Deutsche Nationalbibliografie"; detailed bibliographic data is available in the Internet at <http://dnb.ddb.de>.

Acknowledgements

This book arose from two conferences that were held in conjunction with the *Journey to Con-Fusion* project – a three year research and development collaboration between two contemporary performance groups, Gekidan Kaitaisha and Not Yet It's Difficult. Our deep thanks are extended firstly to the members of these companies whose generosity of spirit made for such an exciting and fruitful collaboration. In particular we thank Shimizu Shinjin and David Pledger, the artistic directors of the participant groups and Paul Jackson and Hata Takeshi, production managers for each company. Mr Hata also co-produced the event with Peter Eckersall and was a pleasure to work with. Our heartfelt thanks are also extended to the performers in the project whose personal generosity and artistic integrity did so much to ensure its success. We thank the following organisations for their support for the *Journey to Con-Fusion* project: The Japan Foundation, The Myer Foundation, Arts Victoria, The Australia Council, The Saison Foundation, The University of Melbourne and The University of Tokyo.

We also extend our gratitude to all the contributors to this collection for their excellent contributions and patience in the editorial process. We are fortunate indeed to include not only essays of such high quality but also the outstanding photographs of the project taken by Miyauchi Katsu.

We are most grateful to Marc Maufort, Catherine Closson and Kathleen Dassy at P.I.E.-Peter Lang for their warm encouragement and support. The process has been enlivened by their interest and enthusiasm.

Peter Eckersall received an Australian Research Council small grant for the research in his chapter contribution. He was also supported by the University of Melbourne Collaborative Research Program in his work on this book. He would like to give special thanks to his co-editors and to his colleagues at NYID. Personal thanks and gratitude are also extended to Gekidan Kaitaisha, Kathryn Hunyor at the Australian Embassy in Tokyo, Lauren Bain and the contributors to this book.

Japanese names are printed family name first. The long vowel sound in Japanese is indicated by a macron (e.g., *Nô*) unless in common use without.

Peter Eckersall, Uchino Tadashi, Moriyama Naoto
Melbourne and Tokyo February 2004

Contents

Introduction

Peter ECKERSALL, MORIYAMA Naoto

Alternatives: Debating Theatre Culture in the Age of Con-Fusion is a collection of essays devoted to investigating the possibilities for alternative ways of working across and between cultural, artistic and intellectual spaces in an era when the reality of globalisation imposes on our worldview. The essays in this book are framed by a three-year long intercultural performance collaboration between two experimental theatre companies; Tokyo based Gekidan Kaitaisha (Theatre of Decon-struction, GK) and Melbourne based Not Yet It's Difficult (NYID). Called the *Journey to Con-Fusion* project, some of the essays will respond directly to the performances while others consider theatre and other modes of cultural representation in-and-between Australia and Japan. A common theme of the essays is the strategic value of "con-fusion," a term adopted by the participating artists in the first place. We concur that such a term suggesting the sensibilities of collaboration, montage and fusion without smoothing over difference is essential for alternative creative and intellectual practices to evolve. Thus, the col-lection addresses contexts for the arts while simultaneously debating possibilities for far-reaching alternatives in an age of advanced capi-talism and globalisation.

This book gathers and considers alternative viewpoints among scholars in theatre and performance studies mainly in Australia and Japan. This is an unusual axis of investigation; an alternative to the more commonplace European-American performance studies nexus. In this sense, the book can address the problem of theorising alternative critical/cultural spaces including the con-fusion of dominant and main-stream critical discourse. The combination of Japanese and Australian viewpoints informed by and siding beside other established critical arenas, widens the scope of the investigation considerably. This is not to say that the contributors are in any way isolated in their critical prac-tices, nor to suggest that they form part of a national school of thought or ideology (*kokubungaku*). Rather we recognise the degree to which education, culture, wealth and systems of scholarly enterprise help to shape and promote points of view. Alternatives must continue to

develop with the result that new and wide-ranging intellectual relationships sit alongside established critical practices and scholarly networks.

Finally, live theatre cannot be translated into text; only criticism,
context and reactive and/or corresponding "lines of flight" are possible.
However, theatre scholarship often interacts with theatre production;
good scholarship and criticism can also be the basis of dramaturgy for a
created event. The craft of research and critical reflection is a creative
lifeline for theatre artists and theatre groups. *Journey to Con-Fusion* is a
dialogue between performance and scholarship where a circular
creative-critical process and faculty might be developed. Responses
herein to the project might be of interest to the artists. Meanwhile the
GK-NYID theatrical collaboration is shown in this book by documentation photographs taken by one of Japan's leading theatre photographers,
Miyauchi Katsu. In this way, we hope and intend that the spirit of the
live project will be conveyed to readers of this book.

Towards Alternative Praxis and Globalisation

Alternatives: Debating Theatre Culture in the Age of Con-Fusion
includes writings by performance theorists and cultural critics who are
broadly concerned with developing alternative critical viewpoints. We
recognise that this task faces particular challenges in an age dominated
by international capitalism and globalisation wherein powerful economic and cultural forces work to erase alternative intellectual, cultural or
social spaces.

The impact of globalisation on regional culture and on theatre arts in
particular requires our urgent attention.

Since the 1960s, the *raison d'être* of contemporary theatre culture in
Australia and Japan has been the consideration of identity. This discourse – which has been a cornerstone of the visionary and innovative
theatrical movements in each place – has found wide acceptance among
artists and scholars as a motivation and a central theme in the account of
recent theatre history. To this end, the 1960s is both mythologized and
critically interrogated as the epoch when a uniquely Australian theatre
was born (e.g. Robertson 2001, Radic 1991). Around the same time, a
contemporary theatre movement in Japan saw a return to Japanese
"cultural roots" – thereby resisting sixty years of modern (western)
theatre culture. This was the Tokyo based "little theatre movement" or
shôgekijyô, described by Goodman (1988) in his seminal theatre history
of the 1960s as "The Return of the Gods". As these brief examples
demonstrate, the identity frame has been a shared characteristic of these
dynamic *alternative* theatre cultures. Nor is this surprising given that

identity is widely valued as a prime factor in determining and challenging cultural values and cultural production (e.g. Hall 1996).

Now a new cultural force has entered the field of cultural production. The regime of globalisation undermines the straightforward relationship between art and culture and confuses the "national theatre" project. To this end, the return of debates about national culture seemingly works hand in glove with a "free trade" ideological framework. The controversial issue of the Japanese national flag (*Hinomaru*) and anthem (*Kimigayo*, see Moriyama in this volume, Eckersall 2001) and the recent "race-card" election in Australia are examples of a cultural turn that sees the economic sphere as global but the cultural sphere as parochial.

This development is short sighted and erroneous. We need to consider globalisation as a cultural and ideological force as well as an economic one as a matter of urgency. We need to theorise their essential interrelationship in scholarship and public discourse. As Jameson notes, globalisation is the "becoming cultural of the economic" (1998: 70). To investigate globalisation then one must consider the wider contexts for economic production; the study of the impact of first world corporate systems interacting with third world forces, for example, and the rise of information economies and associated global flows of images, media, data, aesthetic structures, franchises, technology and the like. These aspects of the cultural economy contribute to our understanding of globalisation and give rise to wide ranging questions about the future directions of culture and society, of ideology and issues such as diversity, equality, income distribution and so on.

In particular, new technologies and mass mediatisation – that simultaneously augment and define the reach of globalisation – are factors that affect the arts. As representations and cultural forms become commodities, they undermine art's seemingly privileged status as cultural source. They confuse the very idea of art and, while they have advanced some sectors of the arts (say video, music, etc.), their presence in theatre and live arts has caused anxiety and confusion (see Auslander 1999). Technology and media have radically changed the nature of theatre production, expectations of audiences, the shape of the industry, the potential and possibilities for creating new work and so on.

Consequently, our attempts to understand the recent history of alternative theatre and the grounds for a politically effective theatre culture itself have shifted dramatically. There is an urgent need for a reconsideration of the politics of theatre in an age of globalisation.

On Invisibility

Terry Eagleton argues that the achievements of radical mass movements from the 1960s are largely forgotten in our time. Rapid changes designed to advance the causes of privatisation and corporatism in sectors such as the media, universities and in the public sphere have blurred the memory of collective radical acts. Neo-liberal/neo-conservative politics and postmodern culture – which Eagleton says undermines the radical view – "comes after the great mid-twentieth-century national liberation movements, and is either literally or metaphorically too young to recollect such seismic political upheavals" (Eagleton 2000: 14). Eagleton's conclusions point to the need to revive, recount and debate the history of and for alternative praxis in arts and culture. He also points to the need for our present-day situation to be investigated with a view to opening spaces for alternatives. At the same time, we are faced with the challenge that the idea and mechanism for alternatives have dramatically shifted.

The fiction of globalisation is that everything is visible. We wish to explore the view that the opposite is the case and many things are, or have been made, invisible. The idea that globalisation makes everything available is largely based on optimistic and sometimes utopian ideas in regard to the field of advanced communications, the Internet and the so-called "information economy." It is true that radical and sometimes marginalised groups such as anti-globalisation networks or the Zapatista uprising, to name two alternative forces associated with Internet activism, organise their actions and have a global reach via the Internet. The fact that such protesters have websites and communicate by e-mail is sometime promoted as proof of the radical potential of globalisation. In response, pro-globalisation media commentators and business leaders scorn the so-called hypocrisy of these rebellious groups. But can we equate the subversive use of the Internet with the free flow of information? More importantly, can we assume that everyone can access information technologies? The fact that the ownership of digital technologies is concentrated in America means that we should be sceptical of media commentary that equates the use of digital networks by groups such as Greenpeace or Friends of the Earth as proof of the innate democracy of such networks. And even in those places where people generally can access digital domains, we should consider the mounting evidence that points to the ways that information is increasingly being owned and controlled by the power of global media forces. The image of a free-ranging information super-highway was only a fantasy at best; a utopian counterpoint to the Internet's actual history as a nuclear attack proof communication tool for the US military. This view neglects to account for the over-all commercial, gendered and American-centric environment of cyberspace and the extreme variations in quality of material. Mass information is not necessarily good information.

While not dismissing the Internet as a subversive tool, it is also important to consider where blind spots might be. We need to perhaps begin to theorise the globalised information economy not in its fantasy sense as a world in which all information is freely available. Rather we need to think about what is absent, invisible, and sometimes displaced and/or erased. In this way, questions of visibility and invisibility take on a new political and cultural meaning. When societies and cultures are invisible in media terms then they are increasingly the location of some kind of conflict, struggle or tension that is deemed antithetical to globalisation's forces.

This is debilitating, especially if one accepts the view that to be without mediatisation is to be without identity.

Media Bodies/Human Cargo

Consider the issue of media invisibility for alien and or so-called enemy forces. Since the first Gulf War, images of war involving American armed forces and its allies have been increasingly censored and directed by visual media specialists within military organisations. The PR machine of war is now a central tool of war. News is to be managed, censored and spin-doctored by a class of highly educated, well paid media specialists. Rather than bodies or soldiers we now see visual displays of "surgical precision" bombing. We see a "point of view" video and data stream transmitted from the nose of a missile that dramatically and silently ends in a video haze whiteout as the missile reaches its target and explodes. We cannot see anything of the carnage, human suffering or destruction that happens behind the TV-static. We know nothing of the people, their causes, and their sense of grief or grievance.

The armed forces likewise identify themselves with their technology. The Australian War Memorial's official war artist chosen to document the Australian forces in Afghanistan reported that soldiers were upset that he chose to paint them in more relaxed poses. As reported in *The Age* (16/3/02), they wanted him to paint the hardware – the machines of war – and were disconcerted that he might miss the central motifs of battle. In the minds of the soldiers, these were the sleek machines of destruction and not the bodies of the soldiers themselves.

For the director of GK, Shimizu Shinjin this is revealing of a larger condition: the loss of human identity and a performing body that is colonised by images of media and warfare. For Shimizu, the mediatisation of bodies has transformed his worldview and his work as an artist:

> Basically, I regard theatre as "war." It's truly war, in the sense that a human body is indiscriminately consumed (in war). However, there was no body in the Gulf War. It was such a shock for theatre, that a war without bodies had raised the curtain of the 1990s. (Otori and Shimizu 2001: 71)

The irony of this observation is that the Gulf War was talked about as the first truly media war that happened "live on camera." Through CNN, which became famous in the Gulf War, we were able to watch the war in real time, as if it was a movie.

Such ideas now seem to have intensified with the result that a new sense of invisibility has come into existence under the forces of globalisation. After the attacks on the World Trade Centre and the Pentagon – that we also saw live on TV – images of the ensuing conflict have become simple and cartoon like. We have not seen, nor can we see complex images of Afghanistan or Iran. We are unable to see either the immense scale of destruction, nor are we able to see human scale pictures of Afghanis or Iranians. Instead, we see unruly mobs, singular images of fully veiled women, and that is all. These simplified images and characterisations are suitable for the plots of globalised media power. Indeed the manufacture of simplified images, that are the endpoint of the reduction of complex social, ideological and cultural problems to the degree that they become like corporate logos or power-point presentations seems ubiquitous. We cannot see in this struggle the aftermath of the daisy-cutter.

Whole areas of the world seem to be largely invisible. We cannot see the Israeli tanks destroying Palestinian houses or the genocidal war waged against the Kurds in Iran. Australian and Japanese indigenous peoples are largely absent from media spaces. The whole continent of Africa is largely invisible in global media. Globalised power and the media ignore it as a "basket-case;" in Japan and Australia, we are largely ignorant about what is happening there. At an international conference on performance studies in 2000, a western scholar and internet-buff proclaimed that we could all network via the Internet. He ecstatically proclaimed that the gathering could take place virtually. The sobering reply by an African scholar, that his university only had two computers, was shocking for the largely first world/north world gathering. If one is not in an electronic network – and many are not – then one cannot participate in global culture.

Human cargo and refugees, those for whom movement across the globe is not a choice are also invisible unless for vilification and political gain. Fuzzy images of refugees being rescued from an unseaworthy and sinking vessel by Australian navel forces off the North Coast of Australia were inverted and used as images of propaganda in the 2001 Australian federal election. The ruling conservative party claimed that these images showed refugees throwing their babies into the water. The subsequent criminalisation of refugees became a central strategy of what has been called the "race-card" election. On the day of the election in Australia (10/11/01) Patrick Barkham wrote in *The Guardian*:

> The prime minister's popularity had been flagging until an incident in August when he refused to let Afghan migrants rescued at sea by the Norwegian freighter, Tampa, enter Australia. Taking the cue, he has emphasised security worries about the many people paying smugglers from Indonesia to get them to Australia. "We will decide who comes to this country and the circumstances in which they come," he promised in a speech reprinted on thousands of election pamphlets.

In fact, refugees are largely invisible in Australia. They are few in number: those who actually land are locked-up in prison like barracks in isolated regions and shipped-off to the Pacific Islands (without irony this is called the "Pacific solution" as the Australian government pays these generally poor nations a fee to take-in the refugees for processing; in one swoop Australia's refugee and foreign aid commitments are solved). Contact with the media is forbidden and enforced by the presence of guards employed by multi-national private security firms and razor sharp barbed wire. The highly symbolic acts of desperate people who are reported to sew their lips together in symbolic protest marking their enforced silence are reported third hand only. The actual bodies of the refugees and their pain are once again largely invisible.

From invisibility, an image of eternal peace is constructed by and for the media. While conflicts and other matters are shown in the media, they are reduced to scenarios in a TV drama. Bush revives memories of John Wayne: "we'll smoke them out of their caves." In this sense, the global media is a leisure industry, not an information industry. Information is a plaything, a toy to be collected and swapped with others. The ownership of the information remains invisible, as does the wider context of/for information dissemination. To criticise this is to branded dull, elite, morally suspect or even treasonous ("un-Japanese," "un-Australian"). This is also a kind of cowboy metaphor along the lines of "we don't like strangers around these parts…"

This book responds to a need to develop and make visible alternative critical spaces and critical practices. This project restates the value of human interaction wherein the corporeal realities of bodies and the cultural experiences of participants are present and persistent. Such bodies and realities might speak back to the mainstream, mediatised points of view. While we recognise the limitations on alternative practice in our age we aim to discover spaces in which a sense of the alternative exists in, and can resist, global cultural homogenisation. For alternative artists and for contemporary theatre scholars this is an urgent task. We intend the following essays to make a contribution.

***

In Peter Eckersall's "Trendiness and Appropriation? On Australia-Japan Contemporary Theatre Exchange" the author considers the popularity of the Japanese avant-garde in Australia and its influence on the contemporary performance scene during the 1990s – problematically the period of a "Japan boom" in Australia when varieties of exotic Japanese culture were fashionable. The essay develops a critique of exchange, noting that such processes were sometimes ridden though with the legacy of orientalism. The essay proposes that Australian anxieties about its geo-political and cultural location are embodied in some of the examples of intercultural theatre discussed. The incomplete and at times polarised cultural history of dis/engagement with the region was a departure point for the GK-NYID project. The essay advances the view that *Journey to Con-Fusion* grappled with the notion of engagement – its histories, processes and theories – so that the participants might better imagine alternative forms of transnational creative praxis.

"Dissident Vectors: Surrealist Ethnography and Ecological Performance" by Edward Scheer investigates related ideas of appropriation and exchange although from a less binary, dialectical perspective. In this chapter, Scheer theorises transnational performance interactions in relation to the context of globalisation and the consequent sense of cultural inter-connectivity. He proposes a model that begins with live performance but inevitably escapes this paradigm and becomes an ecological flow. Inspired by Felix Guattari, he proposes a theory of virtual ecology and/as performance ecology. Scheer's work is helpful in identifying the possible nexus between imagination and critique. The momentum towards new shapes and forms that arise from alternative creative-intellectual flows speaks to artists and scholars in ways that might extend the work of both.

Kitano Keisuke's contribution communicates the sense by which the forces of history and context reassert as potent agencies in the intercultural sphere. "Intercultural Practices in the Field of Theatre: An Examination of Gekidan Kaitaisha's Performance in Hong Kong" discusses a performance by GK at the 2000 Hong Kong Festival of Arts. Kitano argues that larger issues come into play when considering this performance, principally the postwar history of Japan's fractured and difficult relationships with near neighbours, not least the Chinese. In Kitano's view, the idea that globalisation might allow for creative interactions is challenged. He argues that GK's attempts to exhibit a radical or alternative critique of the performing body were ultimately defeated by Japanese cultural history and the transnational flows of capitalism.

If Kitano problematises the intercultural space with geo-politics, then Katherine Mezur's focus on the local and subcultural politics of performance is a meaningful contrast. Her essay "Cute Mutant Girls: Sweetness and Deformity in Contemporary Performance by Young Japanese Women" considers the cultural representations of young girls bodies in contemporary Japanese culture. Some recent theatre criticism in Japan has dismissed this emergent and popular performance genre as "j-junk," however, Mezur argues otherwise. In her analysis of performance by Yubiwa Hotel, Mezur recuperates a critical space of opposition that might resist dominant readings of the mediatised female body. Mezur challenges conventional readings of this phenomenon and provides an alternative teleology for interpreting popular contemporary performance in Japan. We might extend this reading to other critical spaces and the essay is important in asking scholars to pay more attention to the popular domain as well as debating the politics of cuteness (*kawaii*) in Japan.

Mezur reads cute mutant bodies in performance in her essay as a site of progressive politics. Rachel Fensham, on the other hand, considers damaged bodies and/as signs of oppression. Thus, her work relates to ways that performance is struggling to express the commonplace experience of peoples such as refugees, low-wage employees, marginal groups and how questions of race and violence are never far removed from each other and the facts of oppression. Fensham's essay "Violence, Corporeality and Intercultural Theatre" deconstructs the provocative use of racially inscribed bodies in NYID's *Australasian Post-Cartoon Sports Edition* (1998) and work in the GK-NYID project. Her rhetorical analysis of bodies in performance is helpful in locating the anxieties that arise when theatre enacts violence. By engaging with the work of Hannah Arendt, Fensham's essay is a call for theatre to continue the struggle to interpret the meanings of corporeal violence in the social world.

Moriyama Naoto's "A Phantom of Suburbia: Kawamura Takeshi's *Hamletclone*" investigates the relationship between Daisan Erotica's recent work *Hamletclone* and the social condition of Japan in the late 1990s – one that the playwright suggests is evermore violent. In his reading of the play, Moriyama shows how Kawamura represents an emergent sense of transnational identity among Japanese. He shows how Kawamura depicted the dying Emperor to represent a moment of change in Japan and how suburbia comes to represent recent Japanese social aspirations. In this way, Moriyama shows how the theatrical space of Daisan Erotica comes to represent and expose the social space of contemporary Japan.

Denise Varney's "Rhizomatic Dramaturgy: Alternative Performance Practices" looks at ways of "becoming," or bringing into being, alternative models for collaboration in intellectual and artistic work. Like Scheer's work, the essay points to an alternative approach and is not simply a critically rebuttal of the world. It is far reaching in its implications and suggestive of an alternative way for performance studies to progress.

In September 1999, a new museum, which some observers hoped, would become Japan's first national war museum, opened in Tokyo. In "Exhibiting the Past: The Japanese National War Museum and the Construction of Collective Memory" Takahashi Yuichiro develops a critique of the mode of display at this museum. Takahashi examines the ways in which museums that exhibit war may fashion a collective memory of a nation and in so doing points to the various strategies to make invisible the complexity of war and Japan's wartime account. The essay is pertinent to this collection for its consideration of performance as a politics of display. The performances under discussion also relate to cultural history and conflict, and Takahashi's essay offers insight into the struggle between different modes and levels of performance; those that reflect the law of the mainstream and those the seek alternatives.

The Photo Essay by Miyauchi Katsu allows readers to experience *Journey to Con-Fusion* through an alternative medium and enjoy a visual and documentary engagement with the project. Miyauchi is a long-time documenter of the contemporary Japanese theatre scene. His documentation of GK over the ten-year life of the group was recently published in Japan (Gekidan Kaitaisha 2001). In this photo essay Miyauchi shows exceptional insight into the confusion of bodies that featured in the creative achievements of the project overall.

Prior to the photos is a commentary titled "*Journey to Con-Fusion*: Between Australia and Japan" from the critic Nishidô Kôjin. An alternative to the academic essays, this response is a transcript of

Nishidô's contribution to the discussion that followed the performance in Tokyo. Along with the photos, we intend that this will help give presence to the *Journey to Con-Fusion* project in this book and widen the scope of its analysis.

Finally, Uchino Tadashi's "Afterword" draws the book to a close. His discussion of the project in relation to what he terms the emergent sense of "globality" in the world today identifies ways that this book might productively discuss our situation post 9.11. His "intra-cultural" rethinking of globalisation as the politics of globality helps to contextualise the work in this book, while also providing a new cultural framework for future research.

Closing

The *Journey to Con-Fusion* project is a creative research project for the consideration of new possibilities in transnational collaborative practice. In particular, the realities of cultural difference and subjective modes of being impinge on the project and have been central themes of the project's overall activities. The strategic realisation and embodiment in performance of a double confusion/fusion way of thinking therefore lies at the heart of an alternative praxis in the present age. Thus, the project itself is discussed in ways that might shed light on alternative models for collaboration, while these strategies are simultaneously investigated for their value as counter-strategies to the general collapse of the alternative in aesthetics and critical discourse.

This is a study that investigates theatre in the context of culture, thus looking at facets of Japanese and Australian social and political experience in the contemporary world. It reinforces the point that theatre offers a diversity of social and cultural interactions and that alternatives that are sought or discovered in the theatre might impact on, or extend into, other critical and political spaces. The *Journey to Con-Fusion* project, and the scholarship that has been done in the light of this project, is generally speaking motivated by a common desire among the contributors to discover alternative ways of working and being.

Works Cited

Auslander, Phillip. *Liveness: Performance in a Mediatised Culture.* London and New York: Routledge, 1999.

Eagleton, Terry. *The Idea of Culture.* London: Blackwell, 2000.

Eckersall, Peter. "Intercultural Theatre in the Context of Cultural Pluralism." *Globalisation and the Live Performing Arts Conference Papers.* Melbourne: Monash Theatre Papers, 2001. 111-17.

Goodman, David. *Japanese Drama and Culture in the 1960s: The Return of the Gods.* Armonk: M. E. Sharpe, 1988.

Gekidan Kaitaisha. eds. *Theatre of Deconstruction.* Tokyo: Kaitaisha, 2001.

Hall, Stuart. "The Question of Cultural Identity." *Modernity,* eds. S. Hall *et al.* London: Blackwell, 1996.

Jameson, Fredric. "Notes on Globalisation as a Philosophical Issue." *The Cultures of Globalisation,* eds. F. Jameson and M. Miyoshi. Durham and London: Duke U. P.. 1998.

Otori Hidenaga and Shimizu Shinjin. "The Birth of Theatre and the Besieged Body: A Strategy for Globalisation." *Theatre of Deconstruction,* eds. Gekidan Kaitaisha. Tokyo: Kaitaisha, 2001.

Radic, Len. *The State of Play.* Melbourne: Penguin, 1991.

Robertson, Tim *The Pram Factory.* Melbourne: M. U. P., 2001.

CHAPTER 1

Trendiness and Appropriation?
On Australia-Japan Contemporary
Theatre Exchange

Peter ECKERSALL

> Orientalism could never be characterised
> as an attitude that neglects the other but
> one as that which exists within the
> aesthetic exceptionalization of the other.
> (Karatani 1998: 153)

Introduction

This chapter documents the recent history of contemporary theatre and performance exchange between Australia and Japan. It reflects on a category of artistic expression that is diverse and includes post-1960s "new wave" theatres, avant-garde and experimental performance, contemporary dance, performance art, *Butô* and the hybrid mixing of artistic practices such as performative forays into visual and media arts.

It is well known that such contemporary arts practices have often grown from a long and at times problematic engagement with notions of otherness. For example, ideas about the practice of interculturalism in the theatre date from at least the early-mid twentieth century and an interest in Asian performance genres by such influential artists as Antonin Artaud and Bertolt Brecht. Subsequently, such engagements have come under investigation (e.g. Bharucha 1990, Fischer-Lichte 1996) and have sometimes evidenced unequal power relations and trendiness.

In fact, since Edward Said published his influential critique, *Orientalism* (1978) that historicises the colonisation project from the point of view of a post-colonial mindset, intercultural relations have been problematised and subject to analysis. Said's work has shown that artistic exchange evidences the deeper substance of power relations; an exchange of power that displays inequalities and often overlooks or is blind to the consideration of a politics of cultural exchange. The power to choose and selectively appropriate forms without giving attention to context or content is evidence of this, as is a continued wilful ignorance or selective stereotyping of another's culture. As subjects who have moved through and are influenced by the terrain of our cultural experience, we often seek to exceptionalise the experience of another and hermetically contain it within a more limited, aesthetic and stereo-typic viewpoint. As Karatani Kôjin shows: "The aesthetic stance (of otherness) is established by bracketing other elements, but one should always be ready to remove the brackets" (Karatani 1998: 152).

Removing the brackets lies at the heart of the problem for the intercultural artist. The question of how to do so with maximum effect and political sensitivity needs to be addressed. In this respect, many cross-cultural interactions have been fulfilling, creative, and socially and culturally productive so much so that there is much to learn from them (see for example, Eckersall 1998). At the same time, ongoing discussions of intercultural practices continue to be necessary so that we might reflect upon the possibilities for intercultural dialogue as well the problems of creatively negotiating and understanding difference.[1] So to explore these themes in relation to theatre practice, this chapter will focus on the period 1982-2000, from when the first Japanese contemporary performance came to Australia, up until research for the chapter was completed.

Although the chapter is deeply interested in Japan and its possible interactions with Australian cultural production, two things work to determine the predominantly Australia-centred analysis that it presents.

The first is the fact that in the field of contemporary theatre and performance, Australian cultural production is more-or-less absent in Japan. The data presented here clearly shows that many more Japanese theatre events have been seen in Australia than the opposite. No Japanese theatre group can be said to be working under the influence of Australian theatre practice, whereas the chapter identifies a number of Japan influenced Australian projects. Aside from a small Australian

---

[1]   Sometimes the terms "intercultural" and "cross-cultural" can be interchangeable. However, unless otherwise stated, I use interculturalism here to refer to the theory and cultural analysis of cross-cultural interactions. Interculturalism is the praxis that intersects with theories and practices of/in cross-cultural relations. The cross-cultural sphere refers specifically to bilateral relations of exchange and is subsumed under/subject to the more political leanings of intercultural praxis.

theatre studies research group in Nagoya, and the single-handed efforts of Australian film and theatre scholar Sawada Keiji to translate and publish notable Australian plays, there is little interest in Australian theatre in Japan.[2]

This in part reflects a wider geo-political reality that governs Australia-Japan relations in general. As Australia's significant trading partner, Japan is more "important" to Australia than Australia is to Japan. Australian foreign affairs interests and various public and private enterprises have, since the 1980s, been increasingly aware of Japan; meanwhile a composite picture of Australia that extends beyond tourism's holiday snaps is little understood outside of a small specialist clique in Japan. Lest we too be self-congratulatory about our broader understanding of Japan, however, this chapter will demonstrate that one of the problems of some of the Japan inspired Australian performance is an excessively narrow depiction of Japanese culture reflecting a tendency towards stereotype.

We might go so far as to suggest that the very notion of Australian theatre be viewed with a degree of confusion. Unlike the long history of English theatre, for example, or the wide dissemination of the American avant-garde, the idea of an Australian theatre is a post-colonial one. Subsequently its "Australianness" is not immediately apparent or easily understood by recourse to a few well-known names of famous playwrights and/or directors.

At the same time, we cannot blame Japan's ignorance of Australian theatre on Japanese theatre audiences and/or producers. Above all, we should remember that Australian theatre culture is contested and debated within Australia among theatre artists, scholars and audiences and Australian theatre is in part defined by a post-colonial confusion about what this theatre culture is comprised of. Thus, even Melbourne's La Mama theatre, the apotheosis of the new Australian theatre movement of the 1960s, was named after a famous New York "little" theatre of the same name. Before a generation of young practitioners were seen in Japan, previous generations had come under the sway of the ideas and methods of European artists such as Antonin Artaud, Jerzy Grotowski, Peter Brook, and more recently, French new-wave mime artists, Jacques Lecoq notable among them.

---

[2]   For example, Alex Buzo's *Norm and Ahmed*, John Romeril's *The Floating World*, Joanna Murry-Smith's *Honour* and Jane Harrison's *Stolen* are published in translation through the Sawada family owned Oceania Press. Recently the situation has improved principally through Playbox Theatre Company touring select productions of Australian works to Japan.

From another perspective, however, the commonplace depiction of Australian theatre culture as young and vibrant, or drawing from a diversity of cultural mixes, should mean that Australian artists will excel at intercultural negotiations and artistic exchange. To a degree, Australian artists reflect a sophisticated and widely supported multicultural social agenda wherein Australians negotiate cultural difference on a daily basis. But this only confirms the fact that a diversely rich performance culture and an effective cultural politics of negotiation and exchange are interrelated. If this chapter is at first less interested in the "successes" that might be said to have resulted from this social agenda, it is because one of the on-going tasks of this enterprise is to gradually refine and improve upon intercultural praxis. In order to be able to do this we must reflect not only on the successes (and why they are successful) but also consider to what extent older colonial cultural values and issues of race and class continue (or have returned) to impact on Australian cultural realities. Against the evidence for pluralism in theatre, we need to acknowledge the historically entrenched tendency for Australian theatre to adhere to naturalism, on the one hand, and to the latest fashionable wave of international innovation on the other.

All this begs the question of how we might interpret the generally (over) confident viewpoints of Australian practitioners when participating in various forms of cultural appropriations from Japan in their arts practice? I will argue that in some instances such confidence is misplaced. Various historical contexts are over-looked; problems with the intercultural model and cultural *Realpolitik* that clutters the background to such projects are detrimental to progressive work.

This foregrounds a second factor for privileging Australian work in discussion here, that of positioning myself in relation to the field of inquiry. While, documentation and analysis of theatrical interactions allows us to reflect on the Australian-Japan relationship as an entity it can also (maybe mainly) tell us about our own time and place and about ourselves. As Homi Bhabha (1990: 4) argues in respect of what he terms the "in-between" and shifting relations of nation-spaces and peoples: "The 'other' is never outside or beyond us; it emerges forcefully, within cultural discourse, when we *think* we speak most intimately and indigenously "between ourselves". This suggests the need to keep in mind the limits and alternative understandings of the "betweenness" of communication. Many times, I have seen so-called intercultural activities unfold with one party silent, or worse still, silenced. Meanwhile, the other party is raving and finger pointing. Moreover, in recent times it seems that public Australian figures in general have been doing a lot of finger pointing and hectoring.

Consequently, artistic productions in Australia are ineluctably drawn into an ongoing discussion of race and racism; experiments that cross borders especially so. Prime Minister John Howard's stated aversion to what he calls "politically correct" discourse in Australian society has reopened a narrative stain reminiscent of the White Australia Policy. Certainly not "politically correct" were comments by One Nation Party leader, Pauline Hanson, in her maiden address to the Australian Parliament in 1996:

> I and most Australians want our immigration policy radically reviewed and that of multiculturalism abolished. I believe that we are in danger of being swamped by Asians. (Cited in Stratton 1998: 32)

That the rise of Hanson and her anti-Asian rhetoric happened in Australia in the 1990s is of concern. That her views were then defended by the Australian Prime Minister in terms of "articulating the fears and concerns and the sense of insecurity that many Australians feel..." (cited in Stratton 1998: 32) might be seen as abrogation of his responsibilities as leader. As we shall see, artistic productions can productively be read against Howard/Hanson-like nostalgia for whiteness and new forms of racism, if and when, the politics of intercultural negotiation are explored.

Politics are also central to debates about representation in the arts. This chapter is informed by Alison Richards' (1999) excellent study of Japan as representational "other" in Australian drama. In my case, however, documentation of Japanese contemporary theatre and performance in Australia, and the evidence that shows how these productions have been a catalyst for a Japan influenced contemporary performance movement in Australia, are my main concern. Thus, I am not looking at dramatic texts but am interested in the conjunction between Australian images of Japan – a kind of Roland Barthes-like imaginary "Japaneseness" – and how these might be stereotypically replicated in Australian performance. I am also interested in Japan as fashion: symbols and referents from the Japanese imaginary that are appropriated, and how problematic this might be in terms of cultural and race politics.

In this regard, the Japan theatre boom was part of a larger Japan-phenomenon in Australia. As Japanese cultural productions became more widely known and disseminated, they became fashionable in their own right. Images of Japan seeped into popular sub-cultural milieus such as the fashion industry, nightclub aesthetics, techno-music scenes, architecture, visual arts, dance, and so on. In this sense a notion of Japan itself came to be enjoyed (and consumed) almost as a text; as a series of techno-iconographic images that in their strangeness and exotic allure displaced the need to consider the complex (and often mundane) realities of Japanese experience. The need for definition subsequently becomes blurred in the popular imagination. As *Butô* performers staged trance-style performance art events in night clubs; as Kylie Minogue performs in video clips as a postmodern electric geisha; as enigmatic Japanese born "gurus" established yoga schools and trance dance classes among alternative sub-cultures in Australia; the whole notion of Japan became more performative and liquid. The danger is that Japan itself; its history, its cultural productions, and its interactions with Australia, are made invisible. In other words, a hyper-real invention of the techno-commodity generation: Japan as dizzy as the bubble economy that powered its fashionable wave.

***

Although beginning this survey in 1982, the chapter will highlight a brief period between the late 1980s and the 1994 Adelaide Festival of the Arts. There was high interest in Japanese contemporary theatre in Australia during this time, to the extent that a "Japan boom" in Australian theatre culture was observed. In theatre terms, this meant that characteristically physicalised modes of performance associated with and emerging from the Japanese new-wave (*angura*) theatre scene seemingly captured the imagination of many of a younger generation of theatre practitioners in Australia. I will argue that this has had lasting consequences for contemporary Australian performance modalities and raised questions about the politics of intercultural exchange in theatre.

Australia-Japan related performances since 1994 will also be discussed with the view to explaining the evident decline of exchange opportunities, on the one hand, and, on the other, increasingly problematic cultural appropriations of Japanese forms in the Australian context.

The apparent limits to a generally accepted intercultural model among the wider Australian community will also be discussed. To this end, I will consider some of the responses of Australian audiences to cultural productions from the region. In particular, the anti-Asian sentiment that lay behind the criticisms of the Asia themed 1994 Adelaide Festival of the Arts suggests that Australia's cultural relations with Japan are far from comfortable. Despite attempts to rethink Australia's relationships in the region and reorient Australian attitudes over the last fifteen years, many individuals and groups in the community continue to exhibit a deep sense of unease about place, identity and the region that lies to our north. This suggests the strong possibility that the presence of a "Japan boom" in Australia's recent past was largely cultish and fashionable. Under these conditions, the discussion of artistic relations sheds light on the larger question of Australia-Japan relations in general, a fundamentally important, but regretfully incomplete, cultural project.

Finally, I will comment on the *Journey to Con-Fusion* project with particular attention to the third and concluding performance work. As my analysis shows, intersecting questions of race and globalisation were important themes in this project. Focus on these themes ran parallel and was interwoven with references to processes of theatrical collaboration in the wider sense. This combination suggests a version of meta-theatre – a theatre that shows its makings – and promises the kinds of un-bracketing that Karatani recognises as essential to communication and productive exchange.

The "Japan Boom"

The data in Table One (following) demonstrates the popularity of Japanese contemporary performance in Australia and points to the "Japan boom" period of the late 1980s and early-mid 1990s. The earliest visit by a contemporary Japanese performance group to Australia was in 1982 when Tanaka Min's *Butô* company Maijuku performed at the Sydney Biennale. Maijuku are known for a semi-improvisation style of dance-performance. Tanaka seeks to discover a sense of spontaneity in the bodies of his performers wherein the performing body may react to environmental forces in performance without conscious intention (Tanaka 1986: 155). The group was also one of the first groups to include non-Japanese performers in their public events (including the Sydney based performance-makers Tess de Quincey and Alan Schacher). Moreover, Tanaka claims a unique association with Hijikata Tatsumi (co-founder of the *Butô* movement). As a later day disciple of Hijikata, Tanaka has a distinctive approach to *Butô* that often seems to sit in contrast with a more popular "transcendental" *Butô* aesthetic. It might be said that his work exhibits raw and less crafted forms, emphasising experimentation. Although it is interesting that this work was the first to receive exposure in Australia, a more conventionally inscribed set of aesthetic practices became the norm in later performances by *Butô* groups visiting Australia. With few exceptions, Australian *Butô* has worked with a similarly limited body of work.

Table One: Tours by Japanese New Wave 1982-1999

YEAR	COMPANY	SHOW	LOCATION PRODUCER
1982	Maijuku (*Butô*)		Sydney Biennale
1984	Tenkei Gekijô (contemporary theatre)	*Mizu no Eki (Water Station)*	Adelaide & Perth Festivals
1987	Byakko Sha (*Butô*)	*The Book of the Dead*	Spoletto Festival, Melbourne
1988	Sankai Juku (*Butô*)	*Unetsu (The Eggs Stand Out of Curiosity)*	Adelaide & Perth Festivals
1989	The Suzuki Company of Toga (SCOT) (contemporary theatre)	*Dionysus, The Bacchae*	The Melbourne International Festival of Arts (MIFA)
1991	Dairakudakan (*Butô*)	*Kaidan Umijirushi no Uma (Sea Dappled Horse)*	MIFA
1991	Theatre ERUMU (youth theatre)	*Bekkanko Oni*	Come Out, Adelaide (Youth Festival)
1992	Dumb Type (performance/dance)	*pH*	Museum of Contemporary Arts, Sydney
1992	Kishida Jimusho + Rakutendan (contemporary theatre)	*Ito Jigoku (Woven Hell)*	Adelaide & Perth Festivals
1994	Daisan Erotica (contemporary theatre)	*Makubesu to iu na no Otoko (A Man Called Macbeth)*	Adelaide Festival
1994	Dumb Type (performance/dance)	*SN*	Adelaide Festival
1994	Hakutobo (*Butô*)	*Rengo (Far from the Lotus)*	Adelaide Festival
1995	Shakti & Vasanta Mala Dance Troupe	*The Eros of Love and Destruction. Rashomon*	Sydney Japan Festival
1996	Shakti & Vasanta Mala Dance Troupe	*The Eros of Love and Destruction. Rashomon*	Adelaide Festival Fringe
1996	Molecular Theatre (performance)	*Facade Firm*	Adelaide Festival
1996	Takemoto Kazuko (dance)	*Peace of Mind*	Green Mill Dance Project, Melbourne
1999	Gekidan Kaitaisha (performance/dance)	*Into the Century of Degeneration, De-Control*	Victorian College of Arts/ Dancehouse/La Mama

Source: *Butai Geijutsu Kôryu Nenkan* (*Performing Arts Exchange Yearbook,* 1997).

An event that signifies such aesthetics of "Japaneseness" more substantially took place two years later with the tour of the wordless image performance *Mizu no Eki* (Water Station) to the Perth and Adelaide arts festivals in 1984. Ôta Shôgo who devised *Mizu no Eki* offered the following synopsis in an author's note when the performance text was published in 1990:

> A broken faucet centre stage. A thin line of water from the spout. The sound of water. The variety of people as they come by, approach, touch the water, and pass on. In this composition, silence breaths as living human time, not as form. (Ôta 1990: 150)

While not intending to lessen the significance of this work or questioning its status, I want to read the work from the perspective of the question of its Japanese style. A sparse and hypnotically slow performance style combined with the dramaturgical mystery that surrounds the silent interactions of actors as they approach and depart from the water tap brings to mind a classical notion of Japanese aesthetics. This is especially so in respect of core Japanese aesthetic sensibilities, identified by Donald Keene as "suggestion, simplicity and impermanence" (see Keene 1995: 27-42). Mari Boyd suggests that in the work: "seemingly trivial events (lead) to a new perception of life" (Boyd in Ôta 1990: 153). Putting aside such positive commentary for the moment (and not refuting it), we might also consider how such depictions of culture become signifiers for a conventional, essentialised and unique picture of Japan in the eye of its foreign audience.

Moving forward to 1987, the table shows the beginning of a Japanese theatrical boom in Australia. From seventeen visits listed over an 18-year time span, ten occur in the seven years from 1987 to 1994. Moreover, the argument for a boom time is not based on number of visits alone; the quality of most of the works touring during this period was also exceptionally high. Among the groups listed are some of the most interesting and significant theatre companies seen in Japan from the mid-1980s to the mid-1990s.[3]

In the majority of cases, these works are the culmination of many years of creative development. For example, the Suzuki Company of Toga (SCOT), performing in Australia in the early 1990s, drew on training methods and dramaturgical concepts first developed by Suzuki

---

[3] This is not only my assessment. The frequency of reference to and/or detailed commentary about many of the groups mentioned above, especially in Japanese publications, confirms the importance given to these artists and theatre companies. See for example, Senda 1997.

Tadashi in the late 1960s. Although Suzuki has long been a source of theatrical innovation, the performance style of his company during the late 1980s and early 1990s was uncompromising and powerful; the fruits of more than twenty years work with an evolving system of actor training and eclectic dramaturgy underpin the excellence of the company's work during this period. In the same era the feminist playwright, Kishida Rio gained prominence. After the death of her mentor Terayama Shûji in 1983 and the later partnership between her own company Kishida Jimusho with Wada Yoshio's Rakutendan, Kishida seemed to have found a striking creative voice. She distilled her experience of the theatrical innovations of the past fifteen years into a materialist-feminist dramaturgy that was widely admired. The award winning *Ito Jigoku* (Woven Hell), a major work by Kishida and performed by the combined theatrical groups was subsequently seen at the Adelaide Festival in 1992.[4] Major *Butô* groups including Dairakudakan, Hakutobo and Sankai Juku all gained prominence in the 1980s. In retrospect, given the present day stagnation of *Butô*, works on show during this period may have taken the genre to its creative limits. In each instance seminal performances seemed to consolidate (if not conclude) a number of important performance trajectories that emerged from the 1960s avant-garde. Most were shown in Australia.

While a different category, groups from the so-called second and third generation after the 1960s are nevertheless equally distinguished. Daisan Erotica and Dumb Type, for example, whose works have been seen in Australia, are not 1960s style *angura* but have in different ways reacted against the established contemporary scene in Japan.

Dumb Type is an art collective from Kyoto more influenced by visual arts, dance and contemporary music, than conventional theatre. In the period under discussion, Dumb Type explored queer culture, political and personal borders, HIV-AIDS and sexuality issues in hybrid video-sound-performance installations; their politicisation of these themes positioned Dumb Type outside the mainstream trends in contemporary Japanese performance. Dumb Type's work is widely known in contemporary arts circles internationally and has had a discernible global reach. Two of their most important performances, *p/H* and *SN*, were seen in Australia. *SN* actually premiered at the 1994 Adelaide Festival before a multi-country tour. By contrast, Daisan Erotica's work has deep foundations in the critique of Japanese society

---

[4]   Kishida Rio was awarded the prestigious Kishida Drama Prize for *Ito Jigoku* in 1985 and received the Kinokuniya Drama Prize in 1988.

and culture (see Eckersall 2000). With an interest in popular culture and underground *manga,* science fiction and film culture Daisan Erotica developed a new audience for theatre in the 1980s. Although relative to the other groups mentioned above, the group is less well known outside of Japan, it is one of the most successful of the newer groups that emerged in the 1980s.

By such a comprehensive list, one can only conclude that Australian audiences have been offered a selection of exceptional contemporary Japanese performance works.

However, if we consider the Japanese groups touring Australia since 1994, we see a completely different picture. The last five years has seen only five tours by contemporary Japanese groups and of them only Gekidan Kaitaisha are exceptional (Kaitaisha is discussed further below). Molecular Theatre was briefly at the forefront of an experimental "absolutists" theatre moment in the early 1990s but is not widely known even inside Japan.[5] Takemoto Kazuko is more of a mainstream contemporary dance performer, and the Shakti and Vasanta Mala Dance Troupe (who account for two of the five listings) is largely unknown in Japan and elsewhere.

This is not to say that there has not been notable or innovative theatre and performance activities in Japan during the 1990s. There is no evident decline in the cultural activities of Japanese artists; in fact, the opposite might be the case. Japan continues to display a diverse and innovative theatre culture. Several second and third generation "little theatre" artists have produced popular, critically acclaimed and exciting work that one might expect would be of great interest to theatre audiences in Australia. Noda Hideki, for example, is somewhat of a contemporary theatre superstar; both his hyperactive playful "bubble theatre" of the 1980s and his more politically theorised and mature work in the 1990s are deeply significant. Hirata Oriza's "quiet theatre" (*shizuka na engeki*) of hyperrealism is likewise an interesting innovation in the Japanese scene, as is the political critique of Japanese society and culture in the work of Rinkogun. All of these companies produce work suitable for touring. Large audiences in Japan, around Asia and in

---

[5] This was a performance genre exploring among other things arbitrariness in/as performance and performance that foregrounds design elements and stage devices. During this period Molecular Theatre developed a rigid and hierarchical organisation of performance elements wherein actors followed lines of movement on the stage and created various visual relationships with design objects. Their productions of the 1990s were usually events constructed around an arbitrary structure of six or seven scenes, each of six or seven thousand seconds duration.

Europe can attest to their high entertainment value. Likewise, there has been an explosion in non-*Butô* contemporary dance in Japan. Given that Australians saw so much of the representative Japanese theatre during the boom, why the sudden silence? Why have we not seen these excellent productions as well?

To begin to answer these questions, we might consider the possible framing of Japanese culture here, a revisiting of Japaneseness as a form of cultural stereotyping and marginalisation. What is interesting is how a certain kind of Japanese theatre seems to have been popular in Australia and why (and by implication what is not popular).

With regard to the boom-time companies mentioned above, a clear preference for overtly visual, fantasy-like and corporeal theatre is evident. Many of the works feature expressions of extreme physicality, dynamically bold, and consciously exotic aesthetic design, a frenetic energy contrasting with Zen-like stillness, and an ironic play with the images and symbols of ancient Japan. Unsupported by comprehensive knowledge of Japanese culture or contextual information about the location of these works in a historical continuum, such pieces may display Japan as the "oriental other," as exotic and strange. Only three pieces have significant textual components (works by Daisan Erotica, Kishida Jimusho + Rakutendan and SCOT). The popularity of imagistic and non-narrative forms of performance here might fit the stereotype of the Japanese as "feeling-based people" who at the same time do not express their true feelings (i.e. duplicitous in the eyes of the west). It certainly fits the western ideal that the intercultural other should be non-literal or pre-literary and pre-expressive. Finally, in many cases, especially *Butô*, the work is highly abstract, thereby tantalising in its opacity. This factor may perpetuate the popular notion of the "impenetrability" of Japanese culture. Moreover, commonplace use of the nudity and sexualised images in *Butô* has a context in Japan that makes available subversive and anti-status quo interpretations. Such work has explored oppressive forms of social orientation, inhibition and sexuality. There is a danger, however, that these bodies come to be read through a notion of availability and erotics when they are sensationally depicted in the West.

If we look at some of the responses to Japanese contemporary genres and forms in Australian theatre, we see the possible replication of many of these observations (see Table Two, following).[6] Consider also Table

---

[6]   Not all art works fit the stereotype. As I argue, the measure of negotiation in the work is a factor in its successful outcome.

Three that accounts for Japan-influenced Australian projects that have toured to Japan. The table attempts to note the tastes of Japaneseness that are sensed in these productions.

In considering both the representational qualities of Japan influenced new wave performance in Australia (Table Two) and the aesthetic qualities of Australian works that have toured to Japan (Table Three) one observes the heavy imprint of two genres, *Butô* and the Suzuki Performance training. The apparent ease of transference and basic appeal of these genres is interesting. Not requiring language ability in their replication of physical forms, both also respond to a perceived need in Australian theatre culture to develop and expand on physical vocabularies, spatial sensibilities and body-focused *mise en scène.* Australian contemporary performance has been immersed in debates about physicality since the 1960s, to the extent that the so-called "physical theatre" movement is almost an Australian genre.

**Table Two: Australian Contemporary Theatre
Demonstrating Japanese Influences**

COMPANY-PROJECT	JAPANESE INFLUENCES, COMMENTS
Body Weather	*Butô* training system and group of performers founded by ex-Maijuku members[7]
Neo-*Butô*, "new age" *Butô*	*Butô* into/from modern dance, into/from Eastern mysticism
For example, Sidetrack, Not Yet it's Difficult,[8] The Sydney Front	SCOT training system in theatre and performance companies
NYID	SCOT training system in developmental work
Nadoya	*Butô*, Japanese-western music collaboration
The Men Who Knew Too Much[9]	Avant-garde comedy with *Kyôgen* influence
Zen Zen Zo	Suzuki Method (SCOT actor training system), *Butô* influence in training and dramaturgy
Frank Productions	Suzuki Method influence in training and dramaturgy
The Actors Furniture Group	Suzuki Method influence in training and dramaturgy
Open City (Tokyo 2 project)	Tokyo as a sensibility (as interpreted by the artists) as dramaturgy for performance
Training & research in Universities	E.g. Monash University's *Kyôgen* performance (1993), Japanese theatre studies taught at several universities, influence of Japanese theatre on avant-garde directors working with students leading to a broader knowledge of Japanese theatre among new generation

---

[7]   Body Weather is a system of training developed by the Maijuku Company under the direction of Tanaka Min. The reference above refers to a group of practitioners who have popularised the system in Australia through their own workshops and performances.

[8]   The author is the dramaturg for this company.

[9]   The author was co-founder, co-director and a performer with this company.

**Table Three: Japan Influenced Australian
New Wave Theatre Productions Seen in Japan**

YEAR	EVENT	COMMENTS
1992	*The Chronicle of Macbeth*, by Suzuki Tadashi (adapted from Shakespeare)	Performed at the Mitsui Festival, produced by SCOT-Playbox under the direction of Suzuki Tadashi and using his method of actor training
1992	The Kawaguchi Arts Festival under the artistic directorship of Aoki Michiko featured a display of Australian cultural production including: Handspan theatre	Puppet/visual theatre company. A significant source of inspiration is *Bunraku*
1992	The Kawaguchi Arts Festival: The Great Bowing Company	White painted bodies suggest influences from *Butô*. May be characterised as a "world music" group drawing on some Japanese influences
1993	Handspan, *Smalls*	Comments as above
1994	*King Lear* by Shakespeare	Produced by Playbox and influenced by Suzuki's aesthetics and method of training. (As well as the work of Tadeusz Kantor- who is also influential in Suzuki's theatre aesthetic).
1994 & 95	Stalker Stilt Theatre	Popular outdoor visual and stilt theatre group in which *Butô* influences have been evident
1995	*The Head of Mary* by Tanaka Chikau	Playbox-Tokyo International Theatre Festival production of a Japanese play by Australian cast and creative team
1995	*The Floating World* by John Romeril	Playbox-Tokyo International Theatre Festival production of a Australian play by Japanese cast and creative team
1995	TMWKTM	Use *Kyôgen* and *Enka* (popular song) to create a Japan-Australia satire, intercultural satire
1998	Frank Productions	Works closely with Suzuki's training and aesthetic forms.

Source: *Let's Show Japan: A Guide to Touring Japan for the Australian Performing Arts, Arts Victoria, 2000.*

More problematically, an engagement with Japanese histories and contexts of the work is absent in some of these exchanges. As a result, the characteristically complex and postmodern use of narrative in the case of Suzuki Method, for example, or the fundamentally subversive and socially antagonistic history of *Butô* may be ignored. Lacking such contextual framing both systems of production can project neo-feudal and essentialist power relations, the master-disciple relationship, for example. The tendency among younger performers to accept modes of training without question and view actor training as akin to religious training, or guru worship, is a commonly reported experience. Lacking a deeper understanding of the principles involved, some teachers of these methods may adopt modes of inscrutability or authoritarianism, perhaps in replication of training they have received in Japan.[10] Under such conditions, the supposed inability to communicate or express these creative processes in discourse conveniently prevents a more complete analysis of the strategic cultural interventions that they offer. To replicate, in Australia, the interlocking networks of responsibility found in Japanese theatre groups, that can mediate authoritarian forms of leadership, is naive and undesirable, if not impossible. As a result, some actors have reported abuses of power and overblown egoism in Australian led Suzuki or *Butô* workshops. This is not surprising especially in respect of companies that have adopted a "new age" quasi-mystical mode of operation. The martial aspect of training can, when not critically analysed, replicate some of the most visible stereotyped power related images of Japan.

Subsequently, there is a danger that Japanese theatre culture is reduced in the Australian context to questions of image and style if not outright totalitarianism. In this manner, a Japan-like *mise en scène* that alternates between pop-manga, Zen and martial arts comes to represent Japanese cultural totality in the minds of Australian practitioners and audiences. This is stereotypic in the extreme, all the more so for its fetish of the so-called "incomprehensible" and "transcendental" "feeling-ness" of Japanese culture combined with a loyalty ethic that saps individual will. We consequently run the risk that we might be most comfortable with the idea that Japan is premodern, feudal and without clear modes of articulation. We might seem uninterested in their

---

[10]   This is not to suggest that such problems and abuses of power do not exist in western systems of actor training. Psychological abuses that are enacted upon young students, for example, need to be addressed by scholars and educators. The point here is that, as actor training systems, these Japanese influenced techniques rely on a narrow and highly ordered depiction of Japanese society and culture.

modernity (only the glitzy postmodern) and do not understand their political struggles through arts.

The 1994 Adelaide Arts Festival

Annual festivals such as the Melbourne International Festival of the Arts (MIFA), or the biannual Adelaide Festival seem increasingly designed to consume and display the eclectic elements of global performance culture. They combine the rhetoric of community, celebration and cultural awareness with arts politics, bureaucracy and corporatisation. Within this mix, arts festivals might also serve important functions, not just as sites of entertainment but also as instigators of cultural events that would otherwise be impossible in a relatively small artistic community such as in Australia. At their best, arts festivals educate the community of practitioners and audiences, participate in national debates, and offer critiques and reflections on society and culture. Major arts festivals in Australia produced eleven of the seventeen performances mentioned above in Table One.

The 1994 Adelaide Festival, curated by Christopher Hunt had a specifically Asia focus. It was a watershed in intercultural and Asia-Australia relations. Three of the companies listed in Table One as well as two traditional Japanese performances featured at the festival alongside a diversity of works from the region.[11] Five Japanese performance events in one location over a two-week period is certainly a record for an Australian festival. Unfortunately, for reasons that will become clear, this is a record that will unlikely be broken in the near future.

While some responses to this festival fare were positive and the Adelaide newspaper, *The Advertiser* reported that ticket sales had exceeded previous festivals,[12] there was also a strong element of criticism about the festival's "Asian bias" among Adelaide society. Much of this criticism displayed provincial and racist undertones; local arts journalist and "shock-jock" columnist Peter Goers described the

---

[11] All up the Japanese component of the program featured a *Kyôgen* adaptation of The *Merry Wives of Windsor* called *The Braggart Samurai* and performed by one of the greatest living *Kyôgen* actors Nomura Mansaku and his troupe, a large *Bunraku* company (featuring national living treasure Takemito Sumitayo) performing excepts from famous works as well as lecture-demonstrations about the history of *Bunraku*, Hakutobo performing *Rengo*, Daisan Erotica's *Makubesu to Iu na no Otoko* (A Man Called Macbeth) and Dumb Type's *SN*.

[12] See "The Critics Sum Up" *The Advertiser* (14/3/94): 11, and "Hunt's Gamble Pays Off as Sales Soar," *The Advertiser* (15/2/94): 5.

festival as "heavy on the soy sauce." In *The Advertiser*, he wrote: The 1994 Adelaide Festival will sink without a trace. It was a bonsai festival; stunted, spindly, flimsy, rooted, retentive." (Goers 1994: 11)

Elizabeth Silsbury's piece in the same newspaper led with the headline: "Hunt's punt out of tune" (Silsbury 1994). A letter to the editor suggested that:

> Mr Hunt has provided Adelaide with a very selective and ... one sided program of esoteric and generally incomprehensible items which appeal to very few and the exaggerated accent on Asian content has arrogantly ignored the artistic preferences of many thousands who are more comfortable with a Western/classical orientation." (Letter 1994: 14)

Not all responses were so transparently anxious about the supposedly shifting cultural grounds the loss of a "western-classical orientation," although a question remains as to why Goers continues to receive support in mainstream media outlets. In a more thoughtful and critical analysis of the responses to Hunt's festival, *Advertiser* Arts Editor Tim Lloyd wrote:

> Coming to grips with an arts festival out of Asia was never going to be easy for Adelaide. The city has hardly embraced the idea with open arms. Instead, the chit-chat around town, where it hasn't been simply racist, has been a prayer for something worthy and recognisably sound for our Western eyes to feast upon; some kind of grand artistic statement in the traditional Western European style – perhaps the New York Metropolitan Opera, or the Berlin Philharmonic. ... Hunt has run up a real risk that the mood would turn nasty. (Lloyd 1994a: 9)

At least Lloyd attempts to identify problems underpinning the reception of the Festival concluding that small town racism and provincial feelings of ownership over the festival share the blame. Lloyd remained a public defender of the festival program, challenging readers in *The Advertiser* to address their "unconscious racism" and predicting "(t)he 1994 Festival will one day be recognised as the watershed which reshaped arts festivals not only in Adelaide but also throughout Australia" (Lloyd 1994b: 19).

It is evident though that the intense concentration of Asian performance modes at this festival in general went beyond the parameters within which Adelaide society was willing to engage with even a symbolic depiction of non-western theatre culture. It is also evident that we are yet to experience Lloyd's promised watershed. Perhaps the multitude of Asian images at Adelaide compounded to the point where they escaped their hermeneutic otherness and became paranoid performative hallucinations. Such nightmare images, that lie deep in the Australian psyche fermenting from almost one hundred years of fearing

Asia: "check under your beds" as our forefathers warned us as children. Certainly negative responses to the festival seem extreme given its ephemeral status and reveal a deeper and more dystopic anxiety within Australia about place and its status in the region. Goers' continued employment in mainstream Adelaide media too, suggests a tolerance for, if not comfort with, his balefully divisive race politics.

This reaction to Japanese-Asian aesthetics (there was no acknowledgement of the diversity of Asian cultures and forms of expression) bears comparison to the 1999 denunciation of plans to open the Melbourne Festival at the Shrine of Remembrance (war memorial) with a parade that included some Melbourne based Taiko Drummers. Shrine and Garden officials granted permissions and the program for the festival was launched. A move against the festival's plans followed. Criticised by the culturally conservative radio-shock-jock Neil Mitchell on radio 3AW and by the out-spoken Asian immigration critic Bruce Ruxton (Retuned Soldiers League State President), the issue gained support from many groups with anti-Asian leanings. "Remember the war" rhetoric and an anti-parade comment was even made by John Howard in one of few comments that the current Prime Minister has ever made in public about the arts. The Shrine parade was subsequently cancelled and a second venue for the festival launch did not include the Taiko drummers.[13]

We can conclude that the 1994 Adelaide Festival was an apogee for Japanese performance in Australia and box office and public opinion sensitive Festival directors have noted the negative comment that surrounded Hunt's festival since that time. Australians, one might conclude, have "done Japan." Moreover, the nascent roots of Hanson-Howard race hate – with its associated scurrilous fear mongering of the Asian/Middle Eastern colonisation of Australia – can also be observed in this event. Events such as those associated with the 1999 MIFA can only point to the fact that such fear mongering has grown and been given greater reign by the present regime in Australia. This is inexcusable and in the longer term will inflict immense damage on the fabric of Australian culture and society, not to mention Australia's relations with others in the region.

---

[13] See *The Age* (15/10/99) for further information.

The *Journey to Con-Fusion* Project

As noted in this book's introduction, the *Journey to Con-Fusion* project (1999-2002) between Not Yet It's Difficult (NYID) and Gekidan Kaitaisha arose from thinking about artistic, scholarly and professional issues regarding the politics and praxis of intercultural theatre exchange. Rather than focusing solely or mainly on aesthetics, it will be suggested here that the project's artistic achievements are concomitant with its focus on the politics of transaction and exchange in the broader sense. The Australia-Japan relationship and the recognised need for vibrant cultural, as well economic and political relations, was an important factor in the conception of the project. In particular, the desire to investigate possibilities for alternative arts praxis and shape the performance interactions that were undertaken as sites for critically reading world events were motivating factors for the artists involved.[14] Common to both groups was the perception of rising forces of inequality and exclusionary and disciplinary political forces in the world con-sequent to the rise of globalisation. To this end, the project took as its theme the consideration of intercultural theatre praxis and the politics of performance in an age of globalisation.

A component of this approach was the consideration of intercultural theatre itself. As we have seen, Australian theatre enjoys a long history of intercultural transactions and the project was predicated on the belief that theatre is a medium for deepening cultural understanding and furthering communication between cultures in the region. With this in mind, the project aimed to further develop critical forums for the discussion of new theatre practice and hybridity in theatre, and to offer performances of work-in-progress to interested audiences for discussion. Such objectives are also relevant to Japan where, as demonstrated above, performance styles as diverse as *Nô*, "Suzuki method" and *Butô* have been departures for experiments in intercultural theatre.

Given the sense of dislocation from their respective national theatre histories, however (a point that is discussed further below), both companies were not interested in some kind of interrogation of bilateral exchange relationships alone. Current political circumstances in parti-cular determined that this approach was rejected as oversimplifying the complexities of cultural transaction. The *Journey to Con-Fusion* project aimed to explore the complexity of transactions that have arisen in the

---

[14]   As the company dramaturg for NYID and co-producer of the *Journey to Con-Fusion* project (with Kaitaisha's Hata Takeshi) I was part of a creative team that conceived and developed this project through to its conclusion in 2002.

context of globalisation, as it becomes a dominant force affecting cultural production. Among other things, this meant that the sense of a national theatre culture came to be questioned.

The project hoped to avoid some of the pitfalls of past "trendy" intercultural activities. The long duration of the project was seen as an important factor here, as it allowed each participant to develop a working understanding of the other's practice. There was also time for necessary negotiations about the directions that the project might take, for discussing the limits and capacities of the artistic teams, and of the project's scope and content over all. The project also wished to avoid entanglements in the kind of arts festival matrix of commodification and value integration that are described above. As noted in my analysis of the Adelaide Festival 1994, the genuine attempt to expand Australian experience of the world in that instance, through the actions of neoconservative journalists and critics, became reified as a race-based media spectacle.[15]

Above all, I believe that the combination of interests and experiences of the two theatre companies involved were important factors in the project's outcomes.

***

Processes of *making theatre as theatre* in an age dominated by commodity production and social inequality is, for NYID, a way of resistance. NYID have developed a range of presentational forms that aim to show the visceral and intensive use of bodies in performance. Their shows are often staged in non-traditional theatre spaces such as car parks, converted warehouses and gallery spaces. The interactive presence of media and design and dramaturgical strategies that draw on sources such as theatre, popular culture, interviews, history, and media are further characteristics of NYID's work.[16] NYID are associated with

---

[15] It is true that Con-Fusion #3 took place in the context of an arts festival, the Next Wave festival in Melbourne. In contrast to Adelaide, however, the configuration of the Next Wave festival is one that promotes small-scale, artist-produced work focusing on developing alternative and younger audiences. For example, all of the events in the 2002 Next Wave festival were free to the public and debates about the politics of cultural transaction through the festival edifice were present in the conception and rationale of the festival as a whole.

[16] NYID performances have often explored the interrelationship of aesthetic and cultural politics. In *Taking Tiger Mountain by Strategy* (1995) the company restaged a cultural revolutionary Chinese Opera as an investigation of theatre and propaganda. *William Shakespeare: Hung, Drawn and Quartered* (1996) attacked the unquestion- ing elevation of Shakespeare in Australian theatre and questioned assumptions about

an alternative history of Australian theatre and their work is selectively outside of, and rethinks mainstream theatre culture and its modes of production. Thus, for NYID theatre is a source of aesthetic pleasure *and* cultural critique.

Meanwhile for Kaitaisha, the embodiment of a dystopic political landscape and the experiential reality of marginal identity is viewed as an act of resistance to the global reach of capitalism. Kaitaisha are also described as a maverick company and are one of Japan's most notable alternative performance groups. They have worked in various styles since the 1980s and now trace their artistic influences to Hijikata Tatsumi, founder of *ankoku butô* (dark-soul *butô*: a profound exploration of the body as abject and an agency of darkness). Kaitaisha work with physical and hybrid art forms and are a critical voice in the Japanese theatre community.[17] Barber writes:

> The emphasis in their work (is) on an imagery of incessant corporeal struggle – always placed in intimate juxtaposition with images resonant of urban media power and its implications for the human body, for sexuality, and for the spectator of the performance.... (Barber 2002: 176-7)

The common concern to debate social and political events was important in giving the *Journey to Con-Fusion* project a set of aims that could go beyond the typical concern in intercultural work with aesthetic translation and information exchange. Rather than performance aesthetics and the smooth world of intercultural eclecticism, the project aimed to relate issues of exchange and negotiation to performance making itself. The exchange process helped shape the performance dramaturgy that evolved; references to these interactions sat alongside a sustained political critique of world trends. Despite radically differing

---

Shakespeare's universality and cultural authority. *The Australasian Post Cartoon Sports Edition* (1997) combined the speed and exhilaration of sport with an eye to the centrality of sport in Australia as a dominating ideological force. For *Scenes of the Beginning from the End* (2001) the company drew extensively on development work undertaken in the central Australian desert and drew attention to the changing dimensions of Australian space, its relationship to race, identity and cultural politics. In *K* (2002) Pledger has drawn on Franz Kafka's *The Trial* to create a world where media technology and commodity culture have become the dominant forces in society.

[17] Recent performances have focused on the world of post-bubble Tokyo as a ghetto (Tokyo Ghetto series 1995-7) and the nature of power in the contemporary world (*Bye Bye: Into the Century of Degeneration* 1999). One pleasingly unexpected outcome of the project was the interest shown by Australian artists in the work of Kaitaisha. Aside from the collaboration with NYID, several Australian performers have now worked with the company, with Adam Broinowski becoming a regular member of Kaitaisha.

aesthetic values, each group was able to offer the other insights into their creative process while uniting around a common understanding that theatre is in essence a political project. Thus, even given the fact that the groups had markedly differing opinions on the function of politics in art, the intrinsic political nature of art remained a shared perspective among the participants.

Stage one of the *Con-Fusion* project, held in Melbourne, was largely focused on skills exchange and stage two, in Tokyo, on the ongoing translation of these experiences into mature performance (for further details about these events see Eckersall *et al.* 2001). *Journey to Con-Fusion 3* progressed from the notional "work in progress" status of the other showings and concluded the project with a work of rare intensity and vigour (for further discussion of the project see also essays by Fensham, Varney and Nishidô in this volume).

As noted above *Journey to Con-Fusion 3* aimed to investigate the globalising crisis of bodies "in-between" and "in transit." The program note offered the proposition that:

> Airport lounges, clubs, railway stations, detention centres, dancehalls – these are transitory places we inhabit by choice and circumstance. They are public and private places in which we watch and wait, sleep and dream, fight and dance. *Journey to Con-Fusion #3* takes place here. (The project) disrupts the narrative of order over chaos, peace over violence and ceremony over ritual. The intense physical vocabulary and extreme theatrical practice of the two companies converge in their final interrogation of the clash of culture and civilisation. (*Journey to Con-Fusion* program note 2002)

As a generalised description of the possible effects of globalisation, the statement hints at the darker points of investigation that arose in the work, as it became quite troubled by world events.

Con-Fusion 3 came to resonate strongly as a statement of protest to the so-called "race election" in Australia. This election took place in the aftermath of September 11 2001 and saw the conservative party returned after being significantly behind in the polls some months earlier. Many critics in Australia have noted how the election strategy of the ruling party focused almost singularly on manufacturing a powerful sense of fear among the population, with particular emphasis on race anxiety. Fear of other peoples, in particular Muslims and refugees, was used to sway an anxious electorate. The political scientist Ghassan Hage has aptly called this the politics of "paranoid nationalism" (Hage 2003). A theatricalised, quasi-hysterical sloganeering designed to criminalise and depersonalise recently arriving (and turned-away) boats of refugees, and the cry of the Australian Prime Minister that "we will decide who comes here" were sets of contextual references for the production (see Marr & Wilkinson 2003). That the manufacture of race anxiety might be concomitant with what has been termed the hegemony of "empire,"[18] was something that the project aimed to explore. In artistic terms the question might be: When power has become a mediascape of representations, violent performative acts, and staged lessons in discipline and fear – where is the alternative space, what can the artistic response offer?

NYID's response can be observed in their creation of modes of protest and resistance that, in the manner of *gestus* or politically charged representation, referred to the events unfolding in the public domain. By contrast, Kaitaisha, who see themselves existing outside of Japanese culture and position themselves as refugees (see Nishidô in this book); in working in Australia, came to feel their outsider status in a cultural context that was exhibiting xenophobic tendencies. Their sense of being apart was doubled and intensified by the Australian experience. Both companies saw a profound irony in the rise of refugee bodies parallel to and concomitant with the rise of globalisation's Empire like power.

Journey to Con-Fusion 3 explored these questions through the performing body. At a symposium during the Melbourne season of *Con-Fusion 3* the critic Jonathan Marshall suggested:

> This production creates a sense of revivified corpses, of barely sensitive bodies and people struggling to find a natural rhythm or emotional relationship to the other characters that they share the space with. (Marshall 2002)

His comments refer to the opening scene of the performance that depicted a waiting room. Performers made rapid and dangerous advances across the space; they twitched, stalked others, were spun around and fell. As marginal bodies and undesirable classes are ceaselessly moved on, so they might internalise a life of endless movement.

Towards the end of the sequence, two men embraced in an exhausted moment of intimacy. They danced, and then slowly and carefully one actor (Greg Ulfan) walked the other (Kumamoto Kenjiro) to the side of the space. Carefully and almost lovingly, Ulfan faced Kumamoto off against the wall. Without warning he then shocking propelled Kumamoto's body into the wall – thwack! Kumamoto's body crumpled. In the following silence, Ulfan gently walked towards Kumamoto. He

---

[18]   Hardt and Negri's *Empire* (2000) is a critique of the politics of globalisation that argues that the rise of global capitalism, media, American hegemony, and the decline of civil society are interconnected and form the basis of a new modality of power, a new empire.

picked him up. Cradling him like a baby as if to say, "you pain is my pain" (a chant that is present throughout Pledger's 2002 work *K*), Ulfan tenderly caressed Kumamoto's hair and comforted him as one might comfort an injured bird. He then "compassionately" propelled Kumamoto's lifeless body once more into the wall. Suddenly, at ear-splitting volume, a song by the popular 1960s Australian folk group The Seekers played. Called *A World of Our Own* it features the lyrics:

> We'll build a world of our own that no one else can share. All our sorrows we'll leave far behind us there. And I know you will find there'll be peace of mind. When we live in a world of our own. (Words and Music by Tom Springfield. Performed by The Seekers, 1965)

As this ironic anthem to isolationism played, all the bodies began to throw each other against the walls of the space. What began as a singular, painful and careful act was transformed into a carnival release of Australian race-passions. The Seekers were a 1960s clean-cut folk group; one of their members later became a conservative politician. Their use here proposes a bitterly ironic comment on old-world conservative forces unleashed with newfound energy and moral abandon. The reach of these forces though is now propelled across borders by globalisation's dystopic forms and compounded by hypocrisy. Like the fact of locking refugees in solitary confinement and then sending a doctor to determine that the patient is traumatised, the wall banging was a presentational event. The piece was saying: "run with us into the wall" – or be seen as an outsider and face disciplinary sanctions.

Pledger's representational and gestic reading of the refugee body here was matched by Shimizu's abstracted sense of political and identity crisis. Shimizu states that he intends that Kaitaisha be "based on an acute criticism of society which ... translate(s) to social issues including racism, identity in the refugee context, political pretension and hypocrisy" (as cited in Barber 2002: 178-9). Whereas NYID have advanced a theatre of polemical critique through representational dramaturgy, Kaitaisha perhaps internalise the political and investigate the crisis for the body itself that has arisen in society, as they understand it to now be. In Kaitaisha, bodies seem to be occupied by invisible forces and ridden over by symbols of domination and control; performers intentionally and confrontationally place themselves in situations of extreme physical excess and even pain.

We see this in a later sequence from *Con-Fusion 3* when a female performer (Aota Reiko) dressed in high heels and a g-string entered the space, her hands handcuffed behind her back. She violently rolled herself across the floor. She flayed her body around the space seemingly unable to find resolution or closure through her actions. The performance became emotionally painful for the audience to watch. A symbol of sex workers as global commodities perhaps, but also the scene might be read as an internalised commentary on the deeper lack of connection and sensation that the body might experience in the contemporary world; the body as a condition of globality. We might see the body as "sex-meat" commodity and "sex-refugee," bodies that are smuggled across terrains and exploited for profit and power. Pain is shown as a kind of reality, perhaps the final reality of this world; when Kaitaisha use the term "phantom pain" to describe their work they remind us of the spectre of capitalism in postmodern form – empty pain, the regime of disciplinary functions shaping our lives. If this reading of the performance is accurate, it is because Kaitaisha performers commit to the experience of dispossession and marginality in their daily confrontation with the totality of capitalist representation and the system of art as commodity production. They propose a radical view: theatre beyond theatre and the body beyond representational possibilities; the theatrical mode is resisted seemingly through the invigoration and capacities of the marginal Kaitaisha body-flesh.

The accumulation and transference of forms and practices observable in the *Journey to Con-Fusion* project was a measure of its success. In the development of the project, one could see the ways that each group began to address and apply the other's styles and concerns. The affect of one company's work on the bodies and training schemata of the members of the other group was one visible outcome. Although a signature of NYID, Pledger's use of physical assault was, until this project, descriptive and performative (see Fensham in this book). In the waiting room sequence, we can observe the imprint of Kaitaisha's visceral "pain as reality" approach in a relational state with NYID's formal gestic sense of composition. A further circularity of possibilities was opened as Kaitaisha began to develop representational and textual references from the collaboration that were previously absent from their work.

The project was also insightful for its points of disagreement and display of difference. As Vanessa Rowell's review noted:

> In *Confusion #3* the companies create a unique time-in-space through intense physicality, prepared movement and various tensions. Neither company has banished their cultural viewpoint in the search to find cohesion. Instead of attempting to reconcile their contrasting body vocabularies they are, rather, observed. ... By the end of the work there is an undeniable sense that the performers are trapped; hostages to the space, their bodies and their cultures. (Rowell 2002)

Shimizu was perhaps the most explicit about the need to show in the performance "our differences" in the face of the disciplinary sameness associated with the rise of a politics of paranoid nationalism. In a world divided between the singular vision of "empire" and its opponents, maybe the only political solution is to show difference. Thus, while NYID's wall routine embodies in performance the contemporary trend towards the widespread acceptance of discipline and conformity, (the greater fear is being seen as an outsider), Kaitaisha's resolute sense of exile from the world shows difference as the site of resistance to these forces of value integration and the depoliticisation of the public at large.

By these factors, we can see that the relational, dramaturgical and representational critique of NYID's performance gradually dissolved in *Con-Fusion 3* into an attempt to experience the political condition of refugee-globalised bodies at large. While this sense of otherness sometimes sits awkwardly with Australian progressive political sensibilities, it goes to the heart of Kaitaisha's work and is a powerful critique of the divided and unequal condition of the world. Thus, a disturbing and troubling theatre of political symbols evolved through the work into a performance without or beyond theatre: a performance without critical distance, where only the pain of bodies remained to speak for our age. For some the artifice of this remained troubling, for others it was exciting. Whatever the response, the location of the performative interactions throughout the project remained the requirement to address the politics of the situation: to examine the modalities and politics of border crossing. This factor, that kept alive *the processes of the event as the event*, made for a successful intervention into intercultural theatre practice.

Conclusion: After Orientalism?

In his essay "Uses of Aesthetics: After Orientalism" (1998) Karatani investigates the appropriative use of non-western aesthetics within the history of western art since the Romantic movement of the nineteenth century. The well-known genre of *Japonism* is discussed at length. Karatani observes that this appropriation of Japanese arts by the French post-impressionist and art nouveau movements of the early twentieth century constitutes a form of what he calls "aestheticentricism." Aesthetics are understood to be "what is seen," without any problem-atisation of the cultural determinations that might influence the manner by which one looks. Accordingly, outward form and exotic sensuality – not interior value or meaning derived from an understanding of how arts develop in their local contexts – constitutes the value of such a notional idea of appropriative exchange. There is no acknowledgment that the notion of aesthetics is in constant dialogue with ideas of culture. In fact, aesthetics shape notions of culture and identity, what Homi Bhabha has called the "cultural construction of nationness" (1990: 292). Such constructive and constructivist acts are fundamental to developing an understanding of who we are and the places that we live in. For this reason aesthetics and politics are drawn together and politics impinges on arts production in profound ways.

Karatani's essay is useful in setting-out and historicising a politics of aesthetic exchange that have been under investigation here. Karatani argues that the European appreciation of the other:

> was only aesthetic, coupled with the intention to absorb (otherness) into (Europe's) own art. ... Such appropriation was possible only under the condition that the artists' cultures were or *could be colonised anytime.* (1998: 152, my emphasis)

In speaking of European art in the early twentieth century and its appropriative relations with Japan, Africa and presumably elsewhere, Karatani argues that it is the other's artistic culture – and not the European – that could be colonised at anytime. In other words, cultural aesthetics drawn from a culture deemed weaker in the geo-political sense could be elevated, fetishised and granted a momentary status; deemed to offer a provisionally powerful aesthetic sensibility. This was the situation as long as one remained steadfast in the knowledge of whom it was that retained real power. In other words, the coloniser exceptionalises and feeds off a singular viewpoint of the colonised, safe within the knowledge that the former remains under control.

But what about the conditions of Australia and Japan in respect of their ability to transact a relations of exchange? Both are peripheral to the great powers and in their own ways more colonised than coloniser. To the extent that neither country speaks from a historical position of great power, neither is able to speak from a sense that they are either protected from cultural colonisation, nor with the sense of security that they are able to effect cultural colonisation.[19] We can find a complexity or ambiguity here that belies the straightforward appropriative mechanisms of the European context that is Karatani's concern.

More specifically, what about Australian theatre culture? The history of recent artistic exchange with Japan evidences both a problematic Orientalism – an unwillingness to "remove the brackets" in Karatani's terms; and a colonised and fetishistic mentality, that in some instances,

---

[19] I am speaking specifically about the post-war era and the rise of American influences in shaping Australian and Japanese political, cultural, and military spheres.

lacks the self-confidence necessary for a truly worthwhile sense of cultural negotiation and exchange to take place. At the same time, I have argued that success might be found when the politics of praxis are considered and included in the processes of exchange and creativity.

This is a difficult task. Present day geo-political realities have further muddled straightforward power relations. The ways that Japanese iconography, for example, have infused corporate and sub-cultural expression alike points to a contested and constantly shifting notion of power relations and identity in the cultural sphere. Japanese society is complex, made up from an amalgam of local and global influences. It is also clear that cultural relations no longer take place singly between nations. The global reach of capitalism has become extremely powerful; issues of culture and identity are shaped as much in the mediatised output of global corporations as they are by local and regional forces. The transmission of culture via images in forums such as the media, fashion industries and the arts (the culture industry) makes culture itself increasingly image-like and therefore insubstantial. Thus, we begin to experience cultural transactions as circular, fluid and promiscuous, but also owned and manipulated.

This sense of complexity is highlighted in the field of contemporary performance, a genre that emerged from 1960s radicalised theatre movements and has remained the major source of innovation and experimentation in theatre since that time. A field that is also ambiguous and promiscuous, both taking its cues from a global arts-festival-circuit "avant-garde" (subsidised by corporate sponsorship) and, at the same time, espousing regional and localised sentiment and addressing important issues of politics and identity.

The integration of theatre within a matrix of economic and foreign policy is also common. Seed funding for international theatrical events is often derived from government-funded agencies, The Japan Foundation and The Australia Council in this instance. One of the reasons that we no longer see a plethora of Japanese theatre in Australia is that it is less financially appealing for Australian producers. All of the aforementioned productions in Table One received funding from the Japan Foundation. Those listed in Table Three received support from Federal and/or State cultural agencies in Australia. Since 1994-5 funding for collaborative projects in the "region" has been a priority for Japanese cultural agencies and this has meant there are less resources for projects elsewhere including Australia. Australia is not included in the "region" in this instance as Japanese cultural policy is twinned with economic and political imperatives to improve post-war relations with formerly colonised states, especially Korea, China, and Singapore and Indonesia.

The idea of a "Japan Festival" or an "Experience Australia" week held in a foreign city and usually featuring a cross section of national cultural output is an increasingly popular one. For smaller nations seeking to make a cultural impact overseas, it is seen as a cost-effective strategy that offers high impact. (One Australian company performing in New York is unlikely to attract much attention, but ten companies performing over one week might.) In such instances, tourism, trade, politics and the arts are combined in a cultural performance that in its self-congratulatory moments (drawing on the anecdotal evidence of my own participation at least) can resemble a weeklong Qantas advertisement. Typically, such events purport to present a cultural "slice of life" of a nation. No matter the form of cultural production, it nevertheless is subsumed into a representational gesture of a national ideal. The "otherness" and exceptionalism of the event is promoted. In respect of intercultural communication however, the inevitable climate of exceptionalism and the work's status as representational national/ international cultural artefact is exposed. Under such conditions, otherness is the draw-card and processes of exchange are consequently rendered inoperable.

Looking at the history of Australia-Japan relations in the theatre it is clear that otherness remains a problem that needs to be addressed. In instances where grass-roots negotiations have been undertaken and an understanding of similarities and differences is agreed upon, (the John Romeril-Satô Makoto production of *The Floating World*, for example, see Richards 1999, Eckersall 1998, the *Journey to Con-Fusion* project, above) otherness is both investigated as part of the creative process and not exceptionalised as a political statement. On the other hand, the historical body of work discussed here has generally not begun to address such questions. Exchange in the majority of cases is unproblematised and a sense of ambiguity or a continued unwillingness to consider intercultural politics is evident. From the Australian perspective, a worrying trend is evident whereby Japanese performance has been viewed as a site of the non-western primitive, as somehow more pure. At the same time (and reflecting our larger cultural ambiguities), Japanese theatre is considered symbolic of Japan as automata, an oriental-geek depiction of Japan as cyber-culture and a potential site of avant-garde theatre renewal.

These images of Japan swing wildly between fetish and disdain. As Australian culture remains uneasy about its geo-political substance, its history and its present day nostalgia for whiteness, the pendulum swings from Asia-friendly (we are one of you) to racialist discomfort as political expediency. Arising from exchange with Japan we might expect and hope for a deeper knowledge, an understanding of difference, a depth of negotiation skills in the cultural sphere, but the fact is that many appropriations remain in Karatani's terms aestheticentric and therefore can only tell us about our own ambiguities.

Works Cited

Anon, "Letter to the Editor," *The Advertiser* 11 February (1994): 14.

Barber, Stephen. "Tokyo's Urban and Sexual Transformations: Performance Arts and Digital Cultures." *Consuming Bodies: Sex and Contemporary Japanese Art*, ed. Fran Lloyd. London: Reaktion Books, 2002. 166-185.

Bhabha Homi K. ed. *Nation and Narration*. London and New York: Routledge. 1990.

Bharucha, Rustom. *Theatre and the World: Performance and the Politics of Culture.* London & New York: Routledge, 1990.

Eckersall, P., Scheer, E. Varney, D. & Fensham, R. "Tokyo Diary." *Performance Research*, 6.1 (2001): 71-86.

Eckersall, Peter. "Japan as Dystopia: An Overview of Kawamura Takeshi's Daisan Erotica." *The Drama Review* 44.1 (2000): 97-108.

Eckersall, Peter. "Putting the Boot into Butô: Cultural Problematics of Butô in Australia." *Movement and Performance (MAP) Symposium.* Sydney: Ausdance, 1999.

Eckersall, Peter. "Multiculturalism and Contemporary Theatre Art in Australia and Japan." *Poetica* 50 (1998): 155-64.

Fensham, Rachel, and Eckersall, Peter. eds. *Disorientations. Cultural Praxis in Theatre: Asia, Pacific, Australia.* Melbourne: Monash Theatre Papers, 1999.

Fischer-Lichte. Erika. "Interculturalism in Contemporary Theatre." *The Intercultural Performance Reader*, ed. Patrice Pavis. London and New York: Routledge, 1999. 27-40.

Gekidan Kaitaisha, *Theatre of Deconstruction (1991-2001).* Tokyo: Gekidan Kaitaisha, 2001.

Goers, Peter. "Adelaide Festival piece." *The Advertiser* 11 March (1994): 11.

Hage, Ghassan. *Against Paranoid Nationalism: Searching for Hope in a Shrinking Society*, Melbourne: Pluto Press, 2003.

Hardt, Michael. & Negri, Antonio. *Empire.* Cambridge, Mass.: Harvard U. P., 2000.

Karatani, Kôjin. "Uses of Aesthetics: After Orientalism," *Boundary Two* 25.2 (1998): 145-60.

Keene, Donald. "Japanese Aesthetics." *Japanese Aesthetics and Culture: A Reader*, ed. Nancy G. Hume. Albany: State University of New York Press, 1995, 27-42.

Lloyd, Tim. "Editorial." *The Advertiser* 17 February (1994a): 9.

Lloyd, Tim. "Adelaide Festival Wrap." *The Advertiser* 10 March (1994b): 19.

Marshall, Jonathan. "'Dance to the Beat of the Living Dead' What's Old is New Again," unpublished symposium paper, "Journey to Con-fusion #3 Symposium" 2002.

Marr, David. & Wilkinson, Marian. *Dark Victory* Melbourne: Allen and Unwin, 2003.

Martinez, D. P. ed. *The Worlds of Japanese Popular Culture: Gender, Shifting Boundaries and Global Cultures.* Cambridge: Cambridge U. P., 1998.

Ôta, Shôgo. "The Water Station," trans. by Mari Boyd, *Asian Theatre Journal* 7.2 (1990): 150-83.

Richards, Alison. "The Orient and its Dis/contents: Images of Japan as Oriental 'Other' in Australian Drama." *Disorientations. Cultural Praxis in Theatre: Asia, Pacific, Australia,* eds. Rachel Fensham and Peter Eckersall. Melbourne: Monash Theatre Papers, 1999, 137-60.

Rowell, Vanessa. "Confusion #3" review, <http://www.realtimearts.net/nextwave/rowell_confusion.html>. 2002.

Said, Edward. W. *Culture and Imperialism.* New York: Knopf, 1993.

Said, Edward. W. *Orientalism.* New York: Pantheon Books, 1978.

Senda, Akihiko. *The Voyage of Contemporary Japanese Theatre.* Trans. by J. Rimer Thomas. Honolulu: University of Hawai'i Press, 1997.

Silsbury, Elizabeth. "Hunt's punt out of tune." *The Advertiser* 11 March (1994): 11.

Stratton, Jon. *Race Daze: Australia in Identity Crisis.* Annandale, NSW: Pluto Press, 1998.

Tanaka, Min. "From I Am an Avant-Garde Who Crawls the Earth." *The Drama Review* 30.2 (1986): 153-5.

Government Publications

State Government of Victoria. Arts Victoria. *Lets Show Japan: A Guide to Touring Japan for the Australian Performing Arts.* 2000.

Government of Japan. The Japan Foundation. *Butai Geijutsu Kôryu Nenkan.* 1997.

Government of Japan. The Japan Foundation. *Annual Reports.* 1993-98.

CHAPTER 2

Dissident Vectors:
Surrealist Ethnography
and Ecological Performance

Edward SCHEER

These observations grew out of phase two of the *Journey to Confusion* collaboration between the two companies Gekidan Kaitaisha (GK) and Not Yet It's Difficult (NYID) which took place in Tokyo in July 2000.

There is probably always an element of what James Clifford calls "ethnographic surrealism" in a collaborative intercultural project of this kind. There was certainly something surreal about this attempt to confuse two publics and two different companies and also something at the same time systematically ethnographic about the attempt to interact with eyes wide open on intercultural theatre. But this concept is useful in quite another way in thinking about some of the dynamics of this event.

Of the many challenges to critical and cultural practice embedded in this concept Clifford mobilises I want to isolate two to begin. Clifford speaks of activating a cultural and political unconscious, of merging dreams and rational projects and developing new syntheses. In these terms the work of GK/NYID develops out of strict and disciplined physical training but features moments of paradox and strangeness, performers losing their choreographed structured movement and staggering towards the audience seemingly lost inside themselves in a manner which suggests my second point under this topic: the staging of the formless as against the architectonic.

In a "training" sequence called "the cube" David Pledger of NYID takes the performers of both companies GK/NYID on a run in formation through the streets of Tokyo. More than simply training, it ironically recasts sports training in a performance situation (a piece he has done in a variety of contexts most recently in the Worlds Fair in Hanover, 2001). The combination of a rigorous shape in a shapeless environment, a jog through the city, reframing the city in human terms, coupled with the unstructured moments of the performance itself suggests a way of thinking about this project in terms of surreal performance considered as a redistribution of the notion of the formless. You might call it automatic jogging, a kind of aerobic dérive. The cube contrasts the formlessness of the body as it jogs with the hard formation of the group just as the surrealists sought to tap the body's unconscious unformed energy as the wellspring of a new aesthetics and a new culture but always in the context of an extant aesthetic frame. This kind of military precision coupled with an ecstatic formlessness of gesture is one way to see how these two companies have found a common performance language.

GK frequently plays with this contrast, de-structuring the body to return it to its apprehension as site of affect or intensity and not as object of desire or interiority. In the work shown in Melbourne Australia in part I of *Journey to Con-Fusion* the company demonstrated a shift between fascistic forms and the almost total collapse of form, between drone like dance moves and obsessive compulsive repetitions and the jittery, fragile edge of gesture in what Shimizu Shinjin – GK director – calls the "neural system" of gesture. The neural system is part Brechtian Gestus, displaying a socialised positioning and critique; part Artaudian "inspired tremor." The performers shiver as in a trance or fever. It is a stammering nod towards ritual after Artaud where every gesture must be re-made to evacuate traces of the in-authentic. Limited use of verbal language also opens up the Artaudian terrain of the work and makes it accessible to English speaking audiences.

There is clearly something other than a pure Surrealist playfulness at stake here. I would argue, again, that it is in between the surreal and the critical/ ethnographic that the true significance of this work is to found. This exchange is not an expression of two completely formed entities colliding in a gesture of poetic futility. It is a question, again after Clifford, of mobilising practices which shift centres of meaning and deconstruct outdated oppositions of East/west, Australia/Japan, dance/ theatre, body/mind, form/formless etc. It is therefore a necessarily fugitive project carried on vectors which don't signify in terms which the everyday "media shower" (Shimizu's term) would endorse. These vectors, disseminating trajectories of meaning, rather than carrying coherent and stable signs of cultural truth, are subtly mobilised in this work. They are not intended as recuperable in the terms of the mainstream culture, either in Australia or Japan. They are produced as a result of an approach which is rigorously ecological.

Butô, Foucault

Ironically it was on one of the runs in the cube formation that the performers first had a sense of interpersonal contact. Louise Taube, the Australian dancer and member of NYID, locates one session in the rain as pivotal in forging a sense of relationship between the companies. She says that the experience of being rained on together united them and the GK ensemble notably "loosened up" as a result. Taube also makes the point that the exposure to the wider scene of Tokyo in these runs opened the NYID performers out and into a shared experience. Shimizu makes the point that GK had done a lot of their earlier work outdoors as a way of avoiding what he calls "emplacement of bourgeois appropriation." (Discussion 2000) Doing outdoor theatre makes it harder for consumers. But this experience became too popular and so around the time of the first Gulf War they "moved inside." He adds, after De Certeau, that the body in landscape changes the landscape and alters the speed of the situation which constitutes the experience of space. The idea that the physical experience of moving around a city designed for use by technologies of locomotion can be a way of taking the city back is of interest to GK's work in *Journey to Con-Fusion 2* in that Shimizu is concerned with a rejection of media, of the full normative, affective and significative force of culture.

He stresses that it is considerations of external force applied to the body that drives the choreography in GK work. The approach in the training workshops of this project involved bringing the outside into the interior of the body and then, having established a continuity through the body, to move the space around the body by focusing on the neces-sary interconnection. This folding of externality inside the body creates a virtual space; an in-between, liminal space where things are not tied down and new becomings can be imagined. This is key to the utopian strands of this work. There would appear to be elements of *Butô* in this technique but Shimizu argues for a divergent trajectory in that while GK, like *Butô* practitioners, are concerned with becoming other in ac-cordance with the demands of the environment, the neural system does not interiorise, and is not image-based but grows out of real physical friction, the contact between bodies which produces heat and movement. GK, he says, does not seek a transcendental, transhistorical position.

Yet this still doesn't entirely differentiate their work from the *Butô* tradition which, despite its interiority, still sought to perform the body's alienation and displacement in contemporary life. The insistence on these two simultaneous visions, one internal and the other external, is also the legacy of the surreal in this work of producing virtual ecologies. If anything the "neural system" develops, in a more systematic and intellectually traceable fashion, the spontaneous experiments and wild feverish improvisations associated with *Butô*.

In this the two companies converge. Though on the surface very different in style, they nevertheless share an approach to gesture based on re-inventing the techniques of the previous generation of Japanese physical theatre practitioners. David Pledger's style is inherently deconstructive in precisely this way. His inflected Suzuki method, the most original use of this system since The Sydney Front (1986-1993),[1] provides an intriguing way of disrupting the integrity of this system while enhancing the effects of its discipline, staging it with humour and intelligence. This is quite contrary to the critics of the company who emphasise the "totalitarian" nature of the "hard-body sameness of NYID actors," or their AFL physicality as one participant said in the forum in Tokyo. In Melbourne Shimizu had referred to Foucault – more the Foucault of "docile bodies" than the later "technologies of the self," in that he is interested in exploring bodily passivity and indifference to the techniques imposed upon it by the imperatives of industry – and to the neural system as the key starting points for understanding his approach. The GK performers stage exhaustingly repetitive gestural sequences in a way which is similar to the NYID method. As Eckersall explains: "each NYID performance typically dissolves into a repetitive semiotic landscape" while Kaitaisha on the other hand stage a "radical antitheatricality" suffused with "the semiotics of violence, aggression, colonisation and regulation" which "is not so much performed as it seeps through the moment and clings to the air" (cited in Scheer 2000). The beauty of the workshop was the intriguing hybrid produced by the Suzuki based training on Australian performers feeding back into the Japanese avant-garde through David Pledger's appropriation of Suzuki's style.

---

[1]   The Sydney Front was heavily influenced by European and Japanese performance techniques especially Pina Bausch and Suzuki Tadashi. Founding member Nigel Kellaway was the first Australian performer to study with Suzuki Tadashi in Toga in Japan. The Sydney Front made deconstructive dance theatre a popular alternative to more conventional theatre practice in Sydney at the Performance Space in Redfern, in pieces like *John Laws/Sade* (1987) and *The Pornography of Performance* (1988), *Don Juan* (1991) and *The Passion* (1993).

Not Theatre Not Performance.
GK/NYID as Virtual Ecology

Shimizu argues that their work is not theatre, not performance, and is perhaps another representation of power and self-identity or expression. But what might this be? What new form might this call into being? There is no readymade answer to this, it is in the making, but one emergent strand of thought about contemporary performance links it with ecology. Perhaps what we have with the GK/NYID hybrid is approaching a performance ecology. Considerations of place and its effects on bodies, rain on bodies and folded spaces, are only a part of the story of this notion of ecology which I take from the work of the late Felix Guattari who argues in *Chaosmosis: an Ethico-Aesthetic Paradigm*:

> The contemporary world – tied up in its ecological, demographic and urban impasses – is incapable of absorbing, in a way that is compatible with the interests of humanity, the extraordinary technico-scientific mutations which shake it. It is locked in a vertiginous race toward ruin or radical renewal. All the bearings – economic, social, political, moral, traditional – break down one after another. It has become imperative to recast the axes of values... An ecology of the virtual is thus just as pressing as ecologies of the visible world. And in this regard poetry, music, the plastic arts, cinema – particularly in their performance or their performative modalities – have an important role to play, with their specific contribution and as a paradigm of reference in new social and analytic practices... This is to say that generalised ecology – or ecosophy – will work as a science of ecosystems, as a bid for political regeneration, and as an ethical, aesthetic and analytic engagement. (Guattari 1995: 91-2)

I want to argue that it is this ecology of the virtual that we engaged in here, producing a new "paradigm of reference" in terms of the traversal of culture, performance and body, cutting across tracks of identity and place. This is neither a utopian nor a dystopian position. A virtual ecology allows for the staging of the unforeseen if not the unpresentable, a horizon for all modes of becoming, performative or otherwise.

In a different essay called *The Three Ecologies* (which are environment, social relations and subjectivity), Guattari argues that there is a need to develop "apparatuses for the production of a subjectivity which moves towards a re-singularisation individual and /or collective rather than towards a mass mediated machining synonymous with distress and despair." (Guattari 1989: 21) An unmachined theatre of rough edged intimate exploration, I would argue, is precisely what he means by such an apparatus and is precisely what NYID/GK developed in this project.

But Guattari's insistence on re-singularisation, in which we become more completely ourselves and allow the other to be similarly uncategorisable, might seem to preclude the inter-cultural moment, the ethological mode of performance, the mimetic transfer of affects and intensities, energies, sensibilities across the gaps in the architecture of identity? Zizek argues that the other can only be encountered when two lacks overlap so we only really achieve transference insofar as we are dislocated, incomplete, in "mutual vulnerability" as Baz Kershaw says. (Kershaw 2000) But to return the properties of each group, culture or individual what is specific to each does not prevent the appearance of the new connection, a new set of shared affects. The formation of a community of those that have nothing in common works against the habits of thought that continually re-install the same stereotypes about the self/other relation. To remain at the level of the extant structure of social relations, tribes, disciplines, classes and cultures is to be out-stripped by history and "mugged by reality" to quote a former Australian Prime Minister. Guattari urges us to reconstruct "the ensemble of modalities of collective being" (Guattari 1989: 22) but doesn't offer generalised recommendations; he just suggests, "putting to work effective practices of experimentation" (Guattari 1989: 22). What better way of experimenting with collective being than this ephemeral theatrical moment?

The ecological in performance is connected to the idea of the ethological in that ethology focuses on behaviours considered as the "vectors of subjectivation" the composites of identity, those multiple forces which create groupings of humans and identity positions rather than the products of these forces. It is the thought of force and not form and is in the line of Artaud rather than Said, if I had to make a distinction. Ethology is the thought of movement, of intensities and speeds and as Guattari says, "the logic of intensities, or eco-logic, only considers movement and the intensity of evolving processes." (Guattari 1989: 36)

Across interstices of being, in the spaces of liminality opened by ecological performance (*Butô*, GK/NYID) an interplay is set up which can't be simply broken down into the points of origin of a gesture or a technique. What matters in this is the production of ruptures, what Guattari calls "dissident vectors" (Guattari 1989: 37) which might be another name for GK's neural system of social gesture. The crossing of the usual pattern, the breaking of the normative rhythm can create that pharmakon of the performative, that poisonous antidote of a virtual ecology in which we might be able to "detox ourselves from the sedative discourse which TV in particular distils" (Guattari 1989: 32) and which in Australia in the endless Olympic moment was and is organised around physical performance of the most normative, spectacular and robotic kind: the cult of the athletic perfectible body merged with the cult of the state and the sickly sexuality of nationalism.

To get at what all this compulsory sport fetishism, even in post-Olympic Australia, represses, involves just such a disciplined imaginative physical critique as this. Something surreal (activating unconscious energies), or gratuitous in Artaud's sense (as in "the theatre should discover its own gratuitous laws" freeing itself from the orthodoxy of representation) but engaging intellectually at the same time. Still playing, but not the same game.

Disengaging from an official national poetics might also involve travel outside one's culture. This project of surreal internal externality or extimacy, significantly involves two-way travel. How else to extend what we can know and experience of our cultures' limits and our bodies' affects? To know them at a cellular level as intensities and evolving processes is to locate the necessity of this work. This is the challenge theatre faces in the twenty-first century which, as yet, only the dissidents are meeting.

Works Cited

Clifford, James. "On Ethnographic Surrealism." *The Predicament Of Culture: Twentieth-Century Ethnography, Literature, And Art.* Cambridge: Harvard U. P., 1988. 117-151.

Guattari, Felix. *Chaosmosis: An Ethico-Aesthetic Paradigm.* Trans. Paul Bains. Sydney: Power Publications, 1995.

Guattari, Felix. *Les Trois Ecologies.* Paris: Galilée, 1989.

Kershaw, Baz. In discussion at Australasian Drama Studies Association conference, University of Newcastle, 5/7/2000.

Participants from *Journey to Con-Fusion #2*, directors and critics, discussion at Morishita Studio, 9/7/2000.

Scheer, Edward. "Australia/Japan: gesture and place." *RealTime* 2000.

CHAPTER 3

Intercultural Practices in the Field of Theatre: An Examination of Gekidan Kaitaisha's Performance in Hong Kong

KITANO Keisuke

The word "globalisation" is aggressively used in every place and in all fields of endeavour. In Japan the word flies like a "magic carpet" in ways that give the impression that it could explain every newly emerging event. A seemingly endless array of intercultural or multicultural festivals, arts programs and collaborations have been organised all over the world with the view of anticipating a totally new era of mutual understanding under the flag of globalisation. However, these facts – and the central role of art in mediating globalisation – do not necessarily mean that there is a common understanding, experience, or expectation of globalisation and its activities that is shared among communities across the globe. In a situation like this there are many degrees of possibility for works of art. It is not simply a matter of affirming and/or negating the intention of an artwork; rather divergent viewpoints in respect of globalisation make the situation for art complex. In this essay, I would like to consider some questions that arise from this problem.

My essay will focus on a recent performance by the Japanese theatre/performance group Gekidan Kaitaisha in the context of a multicultural theatre festival organised in Hong-Kong in May 2000. Performing in a season of chamber works at the Hong Kong Arts Centre called *One Table Two Chairs*, Kaitaisha created an enormously tense and powerful performance. *One Table Two Chairs* was a pan-Asian contemporary performance event that invited artists from across the region to make small-scale works that each used one table and two chairs. In Kaitaisha's presentation the convulsive and spasmodically cramping beaten bodies of performers was so violently intense that the entire audience surely felt some sense of pain and suffocation. In a garage-like space the elegant scenery suggested a possible apocalyptic near future. This also helped to contribute to the intensity of the tension felt among the audience.

At the discussion session following the performance a critic from Singapore asked about the meaning of some Chinese characters that flowed across the small screen of a laptop computer placed on the table during the performance. "I can read Chinese characters, but those characters do not make sense to me," he said. "Do you mind explaining their significance to me?"

The fact is that the rapidly flowing characters were enigmatic, in particular to the non-Japanese audience. As a Japanese critic explained, the characters signified each of the imperial eras associated with the reign of a Japanese emperor. Each era is know by a set of characters; unlike many *kanji* characters, their meaning is not necessarily clear to people who read Chinese but not Japanese. People at the theatre responded to this explanation by nodding or whispering their understanding. In a sense, thanks to this explanation, the performance – which until that point in the discussion had been open to wider interpretation – suddenly became a representation of something related to "Japan." It started to reflect, more or less, on the realities of Japanese society. And the more people began to decipher the images in the performance, the more they began to read it as culturally specific.

I also observed that some people remained puzzled. Most noticeably, the Japanese critic who offered the explanation was in a quandary at having to explain what the performance "stood for." He was afraid that his explanation might encourage the audience to comprehend the performance as representing some essential "Japan" thing. In other words, to what extent should one have to interpret a performance in an intercultural space like the festival as solely representing the society or culture it allegedly came from? Some people wanted to resist reading the work in terms of its distinct national origin. They hoped to situate the work in the creative enterprise of *One Table Two Chairs* and to foreground its wider cultural possibilities.

It is productive to consider why the sense of confusion arose in the minds of the audience. Yet I am neither concerned here with the aesthetic proposition that an art work should be interpreted for its own "beauty," nor with the theoretical question of whether it is absolutely impossible to explain an art work without reference to its context or social environment. Further, I am not interested in advancing an aesthetic argument that the intensity of the bodies in the performance by Kaitaisha overwhelmingly refuses – or escapes from – any reading as such. Nor can I accept the utopian viewpoint that suggests that local/national interpretations of art are outmoded in the globalisation era. Something else is suggested to me by the performance in Hong Kong. That is to say, the notion of cultural exchange in an age when everyone speaks of "globalisation" needs to be discussed. Thus, in reference to Kaitaisha we might begin by considering how artistic practices are refracted by the increasingly internationalised creative space in Japan. This in turn has bearing on the notion that performance exhibits some kind of national standard, critical or otherwise.

A productive strategy might be to analyse the rhetorical assumptions associated with Kaitaisha's performance in Hong Kong, in particular the opinion that the performance by Kaitaisha represented "the realities of the Japanese society" – a contentious point in the discussion. For the purpose of analysis I would like to divide this statement into three parts; the first being "the performance by Kaitaisha," the second the question of "representation," and the third "the realities of the Japanese society."

Japan Today

To begin in reverse order with the question of Japan today: it has been said that Japan is a society that is becoming more opaque and difficult to understand, both to people who live there and people who view Japan from the outside. In the face of complexity and information overload, one tends to rely on easily digested accounts of Japanese society that, due to their opacity, become increasingly nationalistic.

From the economic viewpoint, one can easily see that Japan has been trapped in a so-called "lost decade," a period of a seemingly irrevocable recession. In the political sphere, one quickly recognises that the country has become increasingly conservative, or more precisely, right wing. This orientation is demonstrated by the passing of legislation concerning the national flag and the national anthem. The reaffirmation of the use of these symbols has been a very controversial issue due to the fact that they are considered to be related to the problematic of Japan's responsibility for the war. The question of Japan's responsibility as an aggressor in World War Two has been downplayed. The ruling party won the recent election despite careless remarks made by the Prime Minister such as "Japan is a country of God." In addition, the social atmosphere has been increasingly gloomy in the light of the Kobe earthquake and the Sarin gas attack on the subway by the cult group Aum Supreme Truth. Every day one hears about weird incidents and eerie crimes including a series of juvenile murders by teenage boys. Undoubtedly Japan is becoming opaque.

This makes for an apparently convincing interpretative model: severe economic recession invites a lack of stability in society, resulting in the emergence and diffusion of the vocal right wing.

Indeed within the logic of this model cultural practices can be creditably interpreted in the arts. Thus, the modern theatre (*Shingeki*) makes connections with the social scene. Modern playwrights debate the social essence and spirit of the Japanese society at large. Some alternative theatre groups meanwhile have devised stage plays that explore the beauty of Japanese language and offer an aesthetic experience that might relieve people's sense of anxiety. Other theatres work directly with people suffering psychological problems or attempt to create works that reflect the sense of identity crisis experienced among young audiences. One may reasonably argue that these theatrical practices are more or less conditioned by the current realities of the Japanese society.

In reality though, one has to be careful about addressing the economic, political or social conditions of Japan in simple terms. For example, the national flag and anthem issue has been seen as arising from a perceived need to create a national consciousness, not at the behest of the Japanese neo-right but in response to the Japan-US security co-operation program and its emphasis on renewed symbols of nationhood.[1] What should not be overlooked here is the fact that the Japanese domestic political situation is also connected to the global political economy. In other words the current nationalistic tendency that is offensively visible in Japan may not be the same as that of the pre-war era as is sometimes claimed. The political economy has changed from the era of imperialism to the era of multi-nationalism and corporatisation. As a consequence nationalism has also changed its form.

Similar kinds of circumstances can be observed in the economic arena. As many economists note, the recession in Japan cannot be accounted for in domestic terms alone. Events in the global economy such as the re-organisation of the international monetary and financial system, not to mention Japan's own extensive participation in international markets, effects the economy of Japan. In other words, the recession is inextricably tied to international economic trends and forces. Moreover, the financial mechanisms of the global economy are largely invisible at least for ordinary people in Japan who are unable to grasp its complexity. Perhaps this sense of bewilderment is what constitutes the everyday life of people in Japan. Perhaps this is a more accurate picture of Japan today.

---

[1]   Some critics have opposed the legislation, not on the grounds that it was nationalistic, but that it arose from American pressure that Japan further develop its national-military symbols.

The Performance of Gekidan Kaitaisha

Turning now to the next aspect of discussion, the performance of Kaitaisha. Here I undertake to contextualise their performance practices within the world of contemporary theatrical activities in Japan.

When talking about the Japanese theatre world, one usually utilises an historical frame of reference that includes *Kabuki* and *Nô* as the Japanese traditional theatre, *Shinpa* and musicals as the commercial theatre, and *Shingeki* as the western type of modern play – from which alternative theatres such as the "underground" theatre of 1960s and the "little theatre boom" of the 1980s were derived.[2] It is commonplace to discuss each of these theatres as separate aesthetic entities that have enjoyed parallel and sequential development since Japan's modernisation. However, as has been recently argued, it is necessary to consider not only the separate evolution of these forms but also the structural relations that each developed within society at large.

Thus, Otori Hidenaga's recent discussion about the changing sociological position of the formerly leftist *Shingeki* is significant. According to Otori, during 1990s *Shingeki* began to alter its political position in the broadest sense of the word and align itself more closely with the ideology of the state (Otori 2000: 50-59). Otori suggested that the transposition in the critical attitude of *Shingeki* could be seen in the nature of work produced during the 1990s. Significantly, he also linked this to the shifts in the cultural policy of the government that began to promote Japanese culture more widely. On the one hand, although *Shingeki* had pursued critical functions by posing questions to society the strength of this was deferred by less troublesome programming. On the other hand, as reflected in the changing emphasis of Japan's cultural program, the government began to explicitly advocate the importance of promoting images of Japan abroad, in particular in programs targeting other Asian countries. To achieve this aim the government funded subsidy programs for cultural activities, especially for theatrical activities in the Asian region. Otori suggests that *Shingeki* had come to take on the role of Japanese cultural production and therefore present the idea of modern Japan that the government wanted to promote. As a result *Shingeki* was implicitly accepting of the state ideology. Moreover, this connection was made explicit with the construction of the New National

---

2 Osasa Yoshio develops an interesting argument that one of the most critical problems in the modern history of Japanese theatre is that *Shingeki* failed to establish itself as a social forum, as it had done in the west. Rather its adherence to emotional appeal that was favoured by audiences informed its dramaturgical development. See Osasa 1990.

Theatre (*Shin Kokuritsu Gekijô*) where many *Shingeki* productions are staged. At same time, when *Shingeki* travels, it is reinterpreted within an international cultural frame of modern theatre.

This transposition of *Shingeki* within the Japanese theatrical universe is enormously significant if one wants to consider the underlying meaning that any theatrical events produced in Japan might have. In short, it is getting difficult to see Japanese artwork exclusively as an agency for the critical reflection of Japanese society alone. In particular, alternative theatrical practices now seek as much distance as possible from the "respectable" *Shingeki*-type world.

To develop this point further we might consider the contemporary cultural phenomenon of *"J-kaiki,"* or sometimes called "the Return of J." (See Asada 2000). *J-kaiki* refers to recent trends in Japanese literature, pop music and art that are journalistically characterised by attaching the prefix "J"; thus, *J-novel, J-pop,* etc. Many cultural practices associated with this trend are disposed to employ the iconography of aspects of popular culture, computer games, and childhood memories. The cultural drift is also characterised by the omnipresence of so-called *Otaku* culture or Japanese cyberpunk. One can observe in *J-kaiki* an aggressively nostalgic deification of Japanese cultural history, although one should be careful about how far to apply this critique. These are not versions of a cultural traditionalism despite the fact that the J-culture revels in traditional iconography. It is more like a kind of cultural practice that is concerned with the fact that this country *"Nippon"* (as read in Japanese) can only make its appearance in the desperately plastic-like manner of "Japan;" that is to say, as something only alphabetically graspable and understandable. Thus, some critics have suggested that the return of "J" is an ironic take on the theme of "Japan as junk" (Suga 1999). This does not evidence naïve nationalism but rather a sense of defeatist determinism that desperately stays in an ironic mood and concedes Japan as a fabrication or as junk. Confusing the matter is the observation that as cultural practices are increasingly politically sensitised or radicalised, they tend to be more junk-like.

One may wonder whether the "J-phenomena" can be observed in theatrical activities. As far as I know expressions such as "J-theatre" have not been invented yet. However, one can reasonably argue that there have been examples of theatre that exhibit J-style as a conscious effect or through their avant-garde concern with the question of Japanese cultural heritage. Uchino Tadashi observed in the early 1990s that theatre director Suzuki Tadashi presented a type of theatrical performance that combined an intensified style of body acting inspired by the *Nô* tradition together with *Karaoke*-type singing (Uchino 1996:

76-97). According to Uchino, such performances, while drawing from mass culture, were defined by their avant-garde sensibility of pushing mass culture into extreme modes of expression. Thus one might say that even though J-Junk practices were not always immediately visible there have always been some potential lines of flight toward staging them.

Characterising the "little theatre boom" in 1980s Japan, Uchino refers to H. D. Harootunian's argument for the rise of a "national poetics" in Japan (Uchino 1999, Harootunian 1993). In his reading of post-war culture, Harootunian shows how the narrative of post-war modernisation and progress came to be a key aspect of Japan's self-image. Yet this singular image of development was in fact a narrative first established in Japan by America. Thus, the post-war reconstruction of Japan and its economic growth is shared in Harootunian's terms between "America's Japan" and "Japan's Japan." Using this thesis, Uchino suggests that the euphoric celebration of everyday consumerism in the little theatre movement in the 1980s came at least in part from this complexity of national poetics in the Japanese society at large.

Given the impact of the long economic recession after the 1980s, however, it may be that Japan's collective consciousness is now more dependent on a national aesthetic, albeit in a twisted, ironic way. In other words, Suzuki's theatre was the forerunner of prophesying the un-ravelling of society and the subsequent sense of identity crisis. As Suga notes, since the 1990s Japan has begun to expose itself to global capitalism in its more naked forms with the consequence that ideas of nationhood and culture have undergone regular change (Suga 1999). As a result, consideration of cultural practice as embodying nationhood and forms of identity, representation and critique must be rethought in the light of the complex and shifting trends within society at large. One has to take into account the fact that avant-garde artistic practices tend to refute simple versions of nationalism. However, in doing so, they may present an inverted commitment to nationalism, but in its junk form.

Representation

This suggests the need to consider the problem of representation. What about the suggestion that we might be approaching some universally applicable criteria from which it is possible to analyse artworks in the age of globalisation? As globalisation evolves might we begin to measure the meaning of artistic practice against the aesthetic background of global culture? If this is the case, then it becomes possible to scrutinise the meaning of Kaitaisha's performance in Hong Kong as some kind of local-global (glocal) avant-garde. This is less than satisfactory though and I wonder if such analytical tools are available.

We should keep in mind that many theorists have argued that what is happening nowadays in a geographical area can be linked to global-scale political-economic forces. Thus, those conceptual and expressive means that we have at hand for representing the state of affairs around us are considerably restricted at the locally and/or national level (see for example, Jameson 1992, 1998). On the other hand, such fundamental cultural practices as language resist wholesale universalisation. One can reasonably argue that there are no universally transparent means – conceptual, expressive or artistic – that span the reaches of globalisation. It is true that high-tech media and communications industries offer the sense that one can communicate beyond national boarders, but as soon as one uses these tools, one quickly realises that there are many limitations to the notion of universal communication.

In respect of theatre as well, the question of the theatrical body, as a site of representation is often utilised by critics and scholars. Some of the discussion of Kaitaisha follows this trend.

Yet I question the degree to which the meaning of performances by Kaitaisha can be dissected in terms of the aesthetic possibilities of the theatrical body. Awareness of the body emerged from the avant-garde theatre practices of the 1960s, practices that undertook to radicalise the whole structure of theatricality in Japan and elsewhere. Yet, one should also remember that the avant-garde theatres of the 1960s were not exclusively concerned with corporeality. They aimed to transform the theatrical space in order to bring about political change. In doing so they utilised not only the body, but also the full range of aesthetic possibilities such as design and music. One should pay heed to the fact that even Kaitaisha situate the intensified bodies of their performers within an aesthetically constructed space that includes an impressive and powerful use of video projections for example. One has to be attentive to the ways in which Kaitaisha orchestrates these expressive tools to present controversial images of the dominant ideology of Japan.

With regard to Kaitaisha's use of the Chinese characters, one tends to regard the performance as mainly – if not exclusively representing the realities of society. Thus, the intensified bodies on stage reflect the suffocating and convulsive nature of the Emperor system as an invisible and oppressive power in Japan. This would be a very convincing interpretation of the work at hand. Even so, I would argue that this interpretative frame is not sufficient. Its theoretical presumption of the universal applicability of the aesthetics of representation in reading the body fails to account for the performance in total.

We have already seen that the current rising sense of nationalism in Japan has stemmed from pressures surrounding the global political economy. Thus, the emperor system – which is historicised as the ideology that promoted Japanese Fascism during World War Two – might have a different function now. We should consider that the ideology of the Emperor system today acts to hide the harsh realities of global capitalism. The Emperor system today is the expression not only of the rising sense of nationalism, but also, of the geopolitical status of Japan as a globalised society at the turn of the century.

It is therefore important to recognise that the representation of the emperor system in Kaitaisha's performance is not merely associated with the historical image of imperial Japan. The Chinese characters that signify the Emperor system flow from a high-tech gadget, a global commodity. Meanwhile, the opacity of the Chinese characters and their reception in Hong Kong points to the unresolved question of Japan's "responsibility" for war crimes. I am left wondering if the references to the emperor system screened in the Kaitaisha piece were received with the social/ideological conditions of the old system in mind or the new. I suggest that the former is more likely.

Conclusion

There are many advocates for the importance of the idea of cultural exchange in the age of "globalisation." Yet one has rarely heard how to actually achieve this in specific terms. Thanks to the development of communication technology, we have come to enjoy a utopian feeling of mutual understanding between cultures. Even so, there are plenty of examples that suggest that we cannot really rely on such a utopian model of cultural encounters. There are important post-colonial questions about the discursive power and refraction of art in the postmodern cultural space. When Kaitaisha posed their questions of ideology and power in the inter-Asian collaboration, it was hardly a utopian practice. Rather it was more like a form of aesthetic gambling. I am not sure to what extent it succeeded in realising its aim. But I cannot help asking if a cultural exchange can only be a cultural encounter, not a mutual understanding. I dare say that the performance by Kaitaisha problematises the limits of representational possibilities but to what end?

Works Cited

Asada, Akira. *Voice* May issue (2000).

Harootunian, H. D. "America's Japan / Japan's Japan." *Japan in the World*, eds. Masao Miyoshi and H. D. Harootunian. Durham and London: Duke U. P., 1993. 196-221.

Jameson, Fredric. *The Geopolitical Aesthetic: Cinema and Space in the World System.* Indiana: Indiana U. P., 1992.

Jameson, Fredric. "Notes on Globalisation as a Philosophical Issue," *The Cultures of Globalisation*, eds. Fredric Jameson and Masao Miyoshi, Durham: Duke U. P., 1998. 54-77.

Osasa, Yoshio. *The Modern History of the Japanese Theatre Vol. 1(Meiji and Taisho).* Tokyo: Hakusuisya, 1990.

Otori, Hidenaga. "An Examination of the Peace Process between the Emperor System and the Japanese Modern Theatre," *Jyôkyô* June issue (2000): 50-59.

Suga, Hidemi. "On the 1968 Revolution in Japan," *Saison Art Program Journal* 1 (1999) 86-103.

Uchino, Tadashi. *Merodorama no Gyakushu.* Tokyo: Keiso Shobo, 1996.

Uchino, Tadashi. "Deconstructing 'Japaneseness': Toward Articulating Locality and Hybridity in Contemporary Japanese Performance," *Disorientations: Cultural Praxis in Theatre Asia, Pacific, Australia*, eds. Rachel Fensham and Peter Eckersall. Melbourne: Monash Theatre Papers, 1999. 35-53.

CHAPTER 4

Cute Mutant Girls: Sweetness and Deformity in Contemporary Performance by Young Japanese Women

Katherine MEZUR

> Surely the nation's gaze is more and more focused on girls. Girls occupy a distinctive place in Japan's mass media, including films and literature. What fascinates the Japanese is that the *shôjo* nestles in a shallow lacuna between adulthood and childhood, power and powerlessness, awareness and innocence as well as masculinity and femininity. (Prindle quoted in Napier 2000: 119)

In a banquet hall with three-day old food on table, ten "girls" from Yubiwa Hotel's *Nowhere Girl Episode 2 Poison* are swatting imaginary flies off the gooey decaying food. [1]
"What do you look like when you're in love?
Hmmm, how about this?" (Grabbing her girly partner, they pose like "movie star" lovers.)
Or like this?" (Two more "girls" pose. Other couples strike American movie-star "lovers" postures. Every girl pairs off with another girl. They waltz and pose, waltz and pose. Suddenly one partner mimes choking the other with her napkin. She falls "dead" to the ground. A girl on the stage sings along in a sweet soulful voice, to their murderous waltz.)
"Goodbye Darling,
Until the day breaks, the murmuring bodies fly into the sky…
Bye-bye Darling…

---

[1] The founder and artistic director of Yubiwa Hotel, Shirotama Hitsujiya, states that the title "nowhere" can be read as "now here." Her little girls perform in the space between nowhere and now here.

Let's link our pinkies and promise...."
Girl bodies lay dead about the banquet floor, while the "live" girls snack and
swat more flies from the table. (Yubiwa Hotel, *Nowhere Girl Episode 2
Poison*, 12. 2002)

In her white slip, and pink bows, the Japanese "little girl" drips brilliant
blood from her mouth, as she clutches the telephone connection. She calls
out and pleads with her on-screen American counterpart, who is transmitted
through live-stream broadcast onto a large screen. Blood keeps gushing,
soaking into her white slip, covering her hands, smudging her face like a
child who has played with a tub of red finger paint too long. White on the
edges, red in the middle: Is she the Japanese flag? (Shirotama, *Long
Distance Love*, 9.2001)

On a tiny tent-like stage, a young woman wearing a lacy bra and frilly
underwear carries a limp young woman in ponytails and baby dress in her
arms. She jiggles, nuzzles, and pats the girl, trying to revive her. But the
little girl dangles limbs akimbo, a very dead rag doll. She squeezes the limp
body. She bats her eyelashes. She whimpers like a lost puppy. (Yubiwa
Hotel, *Muse of Shoes*, 1996.)

Three women wearing little dresses prance and dance about a tiny stage with
blood splattered on their faces and chests. A woman in a crocheted pastel
skirt and lacy see-through top with a beanie hat is suddenly slashed by a
screaming mad look-alike "little girl." The victim falls into the arms of yet
another little girl who promptly throws up chocolate blood as they hug each
other to death. (Yubiwa Hotel, *Inori Hataraki*, 2000)

Over and over again I am struck by these cute mutant[2] little girls who
romp and play in dream-like worlds of death and violence.[3] The

---

[2]   When I speak of the mutant or mutant bodies, I am referring to how women modify
their bodies to create a specific image. When something is mutant it implies there is a
set "norm" that is prescribed by some authority. In this case the norm for the girl
body in Japan, not unlike other cultures, is the girl and "not quite" woman body that
may be gender ambiguous, usually small, slim, slight build, and having a waifish
look. The norm is to have little breasts, no hips, and to exemplify a wavy, willowy
quality to the gestures and postures. The body appears insubstantial, almost
transparent at times. Her gaze is that wonderful ambiguous doubleness: in a very
prescribed way she gets you to look at her not-looking exactly the way she wants and
she may also look at you directly and you can't see anything. In age it/she is
somewhere between a pre-pubescent and twenty-five. The mutant draws on the norm
but goes beyond the authorisation to what is aberrant (monstrous and malformed) and
implies something negative and subversive.

[3]   All the performances and art works cited here were witnessed from fall 1999 to
December 2003. My research on Japanese women performers was supported by a

performances described here are from the repertory of Yubiwa Hotel, an all women performance troupe founded and directed by Shirotama Hitsujiya in the early 1990s. Shirotama focuses her work on young girls and women in contemporary Japan. These volatile Japanese "little girls" perform their "cute mutant" roles as an alternative strategy for surviving outside the social norms of wife, mother, or office lady. Takano Aya, a young woman painter demonstrates this mutant girl strategy in her floating adolescent girl images where mountains may grow from a girl's stomach as she performs a backbend in outer space, or clouds are tucked under her skirt and stars invade her panties, or her "space suit" is transparent and her legs are spread wide to an open heavens, her space helmet is an aquarium with fish before her eyes. Cute but strange. The critic Margrit Brehm suggests: "Despite cherry mouth and apparently defenceless nakedness, what Takano commits to paper in energetic lines are not helpless creatures, but allegories of a state that involves a constant process of relocation" (Brehm 2002; 98). In this process of "relocation," the "little girl" dis-locates. She shifts, adapts, and transforms. The little girl body mutates beyond and outside her social role. Her mutations create, play, and violate outrageously visceral representations of "little girls" that offer alternative mappings to the prescribed cultural patterns of young Japanese women.

In the December 2002, production of *Nowhere Girl Episode 2 Poison* Yubiwa Hotel's little girls in their dresses and ruffles, pink cheeks, fake eyelashes, ribbons, and quirky cute gestures, perform murder, suicide, and violent visceral abuse. They also rise from the dead, brush off their ruffles, and dance again to die again and again. Certainly their girly surface pleads for a different reading than the dismissal: "Its cute fluff." (Anonymous *Nowhere Girl* 12/02) In the following essay, I will argue that Yubiwa Hotel's cute mutant girls perform "mutant-cy" that is profoundly disturbing and subversive. Further, I will examine how these women perform "cute" and "mutant" in order to engage alternative "identities" that, through hyperbolic excess, drive artistic and social experimentation.

When I first initiated my research on the transformation of the female body in contemporary performance, I was focusing on how techno-cyber media and its imagery are transforming the physical representation of female bodies. During that examination of female bodies

grant from the Social Science Research Foundation. This essay is part of a book project on Japanese women in contemporary performance.

on stage, screen, and in installation art, I became aware of the *"shôjo,"*[4] or little girl image, the girl-like women, overly cute little girls, and all the girly commodities that went with them. I stepped back for a moment to realise I was trying to avoid this winsome adorable little girl who kept popping up before my eyes, like one of those bottom-weighted toys that buoyantly refuses to lie down and go away. The little girl is not just on stage and screen. She is live on the street, huge on the giant display videos, and ubiquitous in magazine and comic front pages. Her varieties and types are numerous and classified by their public appeal and media. In the following essay, I examine the little girl imagery in contemporary Japanese performance by first contextualising "little girlness" and then focusing on works by Yubiwa Hotel. I will also reference other young women performance and visual artists whose work in video, photography, and multimedia imagery especially reveals the complexity and profundity of "little girlness."[5] These artists' interventions and appropriations, I shall argue, hyperbolically repeat the ways in which this commercial imagery – including *manga* (comic books), advertisements in magazines and billboards, and *anime* (animated cartoon films) – is transforming the physical representation of Japanese female bodies.

---

4   The contemporary *shôjo* performer has her own curious and problematic twists. In the world of the 1990s, Susan Napier states that the *shôjo* is proliferating in anime like *Sailor Moon* perhaps "as an attractive counterpoint to the darker and more violent texts of much science fiction anime." (Napier 2000: 119)

Further, Napier suggests that contemporary Japanese society uses *shôjo* as a strategy for gender containment that speaks, amongst other things, to the complex relations between the sexes, and also a strange censorship of female maturity. Napier describes the evolving *shôjo*:

One of the most interesting of these strategies has been the notion of *"shôjo* culture." *Shôjo* literally means "little female" and originally referred to girls around the ages of 12 and 13. Over the last couple of decades, however, the term has become a shorthand for a certain kind of liminal identity between child and adult, characterised by a supposedly innocent eroticism based on sexual immaturity, a consumer culture of buying "cute" (*kawaii*) material goods, and a wistful privileging of a recent past or free-floating form of nostalgia. This nostalgia, as summed up by John Treat on the subject of the famous *shôjo* writer, Yoshimoto Banana, tends to be "focused precisely where Japanese 'everyday life' is at its most destabilised and fragile…. (Napier 2000: 118)

It is possible that women today could indulge in this nostalgic sweetness of the little girl and literally drown in cute commodities. However, the performed little girls seem to indicate more complex and radical responses.

5   By "performative" I mean that these works have elements of "performance" that dominate in either their techniques of presentation, for example, through video, or giant photographs, or in their subject matter, including narratives, poetic sequences and character.

In Tokyo's youth scene in the years 1999-2000, adolescent girls created an "other" little girl, called the *kogaru*, a term made up of Japanese *ko* meaning "little," and *garu*, (borrowed from the English "girl") meaning "girl." The *kogaru*, the latest version of little girl, is from thirteen to twenty-five years old. She paints on "panda eyes," white and glitter makeup around her dark-lined eyes. She artificially tans her skin, bleaches then dyes her hair, wears incredibly high platform shoes, and sports mini skirts and tight T-shirt in psychedelic pastels. She powder puffs glitter on different patches of skin so she sparkles. She dons hairclips, bracelets, rings, and clutches a tiny plastic purse, all with a cute pastel animal motif. She is a space cowgirl, a pop icon. She is what I call the new *gaijin* or outsider in Japan, but she's really inside. Like the *anime shôjo*, this newer breed is really provocative: she is having sex with businessmen and charging them. Besides buying her body at the department stores and salons, she is also selling it back. The little girl has profound elasticity: performing little girl can be a strategy for surviving as a girl and woman in Japanese society and it can also be a role of self-annihilation or death by preservation. For to perform one must deny age, physical imperfections, and death, besides limiting one's emotional range to prescribed types and degrees of expression.

In these performance examples, I examine the linked aesthetics of little girlness, and *kawaii* "cute."[6] I consider the aesthetic cultural power of the little girl, and how other critics and scholars read the little girl's role in contemporary Japanese society. How do the visceral sweetness, nostalgic allure, and articulated artifice of the little girl icon play out in performance? Do the acts of the performing flesh/meat body interfere

---

6   The spring 1997 feature article in *Bijutsu Techô (Art Notebook)*, a prestigious monthly art journal, was devoted to *kawaii* aesthetics and culture. *Kawaii* can mean variously cute, pretty, cutesy, or sweet. For example, "hello kitty" motif objects are *kawaii* with their pink little kitty icon. Things that are decorated, with delicate frilly, lacy material or designs are *kawaii*. Little girls have a strong hold on kawaii culture: their dolls, their clothes, and now their *keitei denwa* (mobile phones) are all cute. Pink dominates cute culture. Tiny delicate statues of puppies or kittens are *kawaii*. Much of pop "girl" iconography, the cute prettiness of little girl-ness suggests a power to seduce and transform. This cute girl image is the image that *manga* and *anime* exploit over and over again. She is a bouncing little girl, without any past. She can transform into the princess goddess, the elevator girl, or the school girl in her plaid skirt uniform. In *manga*, she is also the one who is most frequently raped, abandoned, and murdered. In *anime*, she is saved for some incredible mission that will threaten her life and force her to submit to some torture that strips her body and remakes it. The *anime* girl is full busted, long legged, and ready for sensual or violent adventures. She is virtual but viscerally cute with huge eyes, pug nose, and tiny chin.

and distort the mediatised body image to the extent that "live" mutant girls then offer an alternative subterfuge to the dominant media/social norms?

This examination of "cute mutant girls" raises questions concerning the focus of the Japanese economy on young women and how its bodily inscriptions serve to enforce an artificial, almost cyborg-like, "little girl" body, imposing a kind of gruesome and creative cosmetic and accessory consumption. In performance and visual artwork, women – mostly but not exclusively young women – execute this image of the "mutant" little girl. In some cases there is a profound sense of depression and self-annihilation about the mutant little girl image. In other performances, the little girl role demonstrates an intoxicating airiness, a carefree, but frothy, sweetness, with a "who cares about the future, live for the moment!" persona and attitude. Between the two extremes there are the subversive and complex voices of artists who I think are struggling to somehow use and negotiate with the little girl image and its most powerful aesthetic: *kawaii* or cuteness.

Among the groups that borrow from *manga* and *anime* and combine cute and frothy with cute and violent, there are artists that claim the little girl as a vehicle for profound subversion and freedom from a set Japanese female identity and others who use the little girl's virtual and visceral properties of nostalgia, eroticism, and techno violence for their own agendas. For this essay I will focus on this last group because I think these "girls" take the greatest risks. They consistently push their mutant bodies towards what Susan Napier suggests is a dominant motif in *anime;* "girls" in "apocalyptic" works who transform from girls to grotesques and back again through "assault, destruction, and profound rage." (Napier 2000: 18) Napier suggests the darkness of these transformations and questions the use of the little girl. She keenly observes the complexity and sophistication of the many types of little girls. I think the live physical performance of little girl roles in a hyperbolic style is the safe screen divide: women-girls, in front of your very eyes become grotesques. They do this, not in simple "ugly" cute ways, but rather by twisting cute notions of child-likeness with violence, pornography and abjection mixed into their girly acts.

For example, in *Nowhere Girl*, Yubiwa Hotel "girls" waltz in a strange girl cotillion. Moving in lines and formations, theirs is a regimented purposeful dance. When they suddenly break up into partners and, in one waltz sequence, strangle their partners with the banquet table napkins and then leave them in crumpled pink lumps around the table. Their waltzing murder act is strangely twisted by the lack of struggle by the victims: they pull gently away and then slump to the floor, while the perpetrators step around or over their bodies, somewhat surprised or slightly disturbed at this inconvenience. At first their strangling looks like a gesture of fondness, a hug. But the sudden tightening of the napkin, and then the bodies going limp, are surprising. Still, their fallen bodies do not really "die" because they get up again in the following sequence. Thus the violence is made strange, and the "little girl" flesh or meat body seems expendable. Do these women perform like dolls, or is it that their "girl acts" are always, inevitably discountable: girl deaths are merely child games? Yubiwa Hotel's "message" is layered. Their frothy surface may be obnoxious, but glimpses of the scars and wounds beneath, bite deep into the pink lacy gestures and reveal the scabs, cuts, and bruises of social abuse.

In a final banquet scene, one of the leading "nowhere" girls, is stuffing herself at the head of the table. Along with her girl friends, she is partying to the hilt with food and singing, but she also wears a noose of thick rope around her neck. The rope has been extended over a high curtain rod on the upstage area. Everyone else is singing, stuffing their faces with old food. She alone is struggling with eating a sugar frost covered cake and getting hung, as the rope gradually pulls her neck back. She expires while softly singing; she chokes with the tightening rope sweetly murmuring and smiling after her last mouthful. Others rush over to help her, as she falls face flat into her cake. These girl acts appear "abstract" because the child-like playing at murder and suicide undercuts the cruelty. Unlike *anime*, these girl bodies on stage in the flesh suggest a deadly raving girl population that has only begun to emerge. These examples of Yubiwa Hotel illuminate the work of young women artists who are negotiating the visceral and virtual "girl" to create new bodies of different physicality, and complex identities. Their agendas are multiple and different: "the sweetness is heart-warming and cruel ... girls can cause great pain and longing ... it's my style, it's fun and alluring." (Shirotama 2001). But all these young women, and especially Yubiwa Hotel, exploit the "little girl" as an alternative to the socially restricted "woman." In their process/performance of "little girl" they de-nature "girl" by making our kinaesthetic senses disengage and withdraw from that fuzzy pink sweetness.

I address the little girl "cuteness" in contemporary performance as an alternative strategy for negotiating for a kind of authority over the bodies of these artists and the content of their performances. In this case "alternative" may be very subtle or outrageous, but it is always a negotiation of the "norm." For example, Shirotama negotiates "cute" when one little girl kills another. Further, young women artists in Japan, under the economic restrictions of the 1990s through to the present, despite those circumstances have propelled their performance agenda: that they would carve a space for themselves in the professional performance landscape created and inhabited by men.

While I do not purport to be an expert on the globalisation of cuteness and cute products, it is a fact that cute commodities have proliferated in many local shops. However, it is a safe version of Japanese cute that gets exported in "hello kitty" products and animation. More extremely "cute" stuff that is provocative and seductive does generally get exported to the west. Japanese "cute" is not limited to the cute of childhood toys and warm fuzziness. There is an adult "cute," which is innocent, guilty, and uncanny. It has the mysterious power of melting the heart and secretly strangling maturity, responsibility, and power. Certainly "cute" in Japan is simultaneously and ambiguously dangerous, insipid, stultifying, and wondrous. Coupled with little girl, the "cute little girl" becomes a transformative icon that is simultaneously loaded with meanings and vacant: an evacuated yet saturated image and role.

At present there are several notable Japanese male artists who are known for commenting on the ambiguous edginess of "cute," especially emphasising its dangerous, even violent elements. Nara Yoshimoto's oversized sculptures of toddlers and puppy dogs, and his paintings of huge-headed little children (with knives and expressions of anger) "stand under the strangely rapt tension between serenity, melancholy, sadness, and angst, aggressiveness and despair." (Jansen 2002: 136). Murakami Takashi, whose work draws on cyber-like girl-images from *anime* and *manga*, featured in a recent exhibition entitled "the darker side of childhood" (Museum of Modern Art, San Francisco, 2001). Both of these artists were featured in a second exhibition called "Superflat" that celebrated the extreme way that the digital visual world has accomplished a two dimensional sense of consciousness; that of "super flatness" linking past, present, and future in an original vision that arises in the global "screen" culture. According to Murakami: "Society, customs, art [and] culture all are extremely two dimensional." (Murakami cited in Brehm 2002: 36) The subject matter of these artists, drawing on cute children (especially girls), toys and *anime* and *manga* characters, reflects a state of "regression to being a child," (Brehm 2002: 17) Yubiwa Hotel's iconography of mutant girls resonates with Brehm's response to the art of Murakami and Nara:

> The infantile characteristics (Kindchenschema) – nature's strategy for eliciting a caring response – are used as a foil to engage the spectator's emotions and to present the insidious relationship between power and powerlessness with reference to this structural contrast. (Brehm 2002: 17)

Both contemporary performances and art works draw on Japanese *anime* and *manga* images of the *shôjo* to an extraordinary extent. The little girl roles in *anime* fall into several main categories; among them a bouncing breasted Barbie Doll, a demure, but still buxom, Japanese uniformed schoolgirl, and a changeling cyborg-girl. *Anime* little girl types are often the original/host bodies of figures that later transform into various "super" women roles, like cyborg warrior women, or super-sexed creature-feature women, or space sprites. These mediatised little girls have extra-human physical powers and paranormal mental abilities making them mutant babes. Most intriguing are the little girls who enact freakish hybrid roles. These are created or bio-technically built little girls who freely morph from gorgeous gangster demons to eerily possessed paranormal schoolgirls. In all cases, some higher power possesses the girl's psyche. The possession often merges technological and spiritual higher powers. In some cases through surgery or "brain change" the form of the little girl mutates into another female-like being that is part machine. The various morphed forms maintain a relationship to little girlness by keeping the cute face, big eyes, or sweet voice. At the same time, they usually possess a "sexually mature" body that has the model body of perky bouncing breasts, tiny waist, long slim legs, and no body hair. While this may appear contradictory, little girl agency combines transformability, ambiguity, and transgression in order to gleefully create alternative, mutant, and even macabre girl bodies in their transformer roles in performance.

The little girls in performance genres demonstrate their transformer roles in the flesh, performing something akin to what Amelia Jones calls the "flaunting of the reversibility of flesh" (Jones 2000: 16). Jones' concept of "unnatural acts" of the intertwining of spectatorial perception with the mediated bodies on screens can be used to examine little girl live acts as well. The braiding of images, and the imbrications of image and flesh produce distortions of the little girl: strange creatures in lumpy bodies, their own mutant girl pop.

Yubiwa Hotel explicitly sets out to exploit the messy body of the *anime* girl/woman in their performance works when performers "die" bleeding chocolate blood, or when one of the "dead" girls is placed on a factory conveyor belt; her body "processed" in their toy factory (Yubiwa Hotel's *Inori Hataraki* 2000). Thus, in contemporary Japanese performance and installation art, young women are creating their own body art that mixes pixels and flesh into representations that distort, morph, and even mutilate their own bodies to create "cute" little girl ones. Using movement, photography, projections, video, sound, props, costumes, and texts, young women in groups like Kyupi Kyupi or solo artists like Mori Mariko are playing "games" with animation and comic book images of mutant little girls. The performers may appear to be cute little goddesses or kinky heavenly maidens but they can transform back and forth from girly-girl victims to Barbie-cyborg warriors. It is these transformations and transformative moments that can be active sites of resistance, or better still, alternative acts that can, depending upon their degree of mutant-cy, disturb, degrade, or even destroy socially enforced images and roles for Japanese women. The little girl stands a chance, if momentarily, to raise the alarm, cause discomfort, and play gleefully with tools of destruction and creation. Spectators have to take the time for a second look in order to cooperate with the reversibility and transformativity that these works offer.

De-Natured Girls

Contemporary artwork and performances provoke contradictory readings of little girlness and cute. They make strange what at first appears mundane. The unnatural acts disrupt and complicate the spectator's seemingly simple attraction to child-likeness. They make strange the "natural beauty" of a girl child. The hyperbolic "cute" acts performed by women de-natures "girl-ness," and consequently disturb whole performative constructs of youth, gender, sex, and sexuality. Amelia Jones's treatment of body art resonates with the idea of de-natured girls:

> The most disturbing acts are those that insistently perform bodies/selves in such a way as to activate spectatorial anxieties and /or desires, while at the same time calling into question what it might mean to call something "natural" (or for that matter, "unnatural"). (Jones 2000: 13)

The opening of *Nowhere Girl Episode 2 Poison* is an example of this "de-naturing." Suddenly ten young women in ruffled skirts and lacy jackets with bows in their hair burst into the banquet room and run full tilt around the banquet table, up and down the aisles of the spectators, screaming and giggling in high piercing shrieks. The women proceed to poke their fingers into food that has been left on a banquet table, licking and tasting as they go. I am thinking: "Here come the GIRLZ! Oh my God, grown women running around like cute mutants." Mutant Girls, that is. I look carefully. I see their enormous fake eyelashes, their thick pasty pink makeup and flowery hair ornaments. They gesture and pose in comic book "pictures": arms, legs akimbo, puckered rose bud smiles, prancing about with tiny tiptoe steps in their high heels. Moving from one pose with a finger to chin, they force a petulant smile or grimace, putting their hands to their hips and shaking in consternation one moment, giggling the next. They squeal with delight over slapping

another girl on the bottom. They appear innocuous, even burlesque or
vamp versions of men in "girl" drag, but taken further – because they
are female bodies beneath – or are they?

As this is my fourth Yubiwa Hotel performance I am ready for the
girls from "nowhere" with their funny girly clothes and bodies. I see
transparently, their mature women bodies beneath, performing girly
little girls in gooey pinks, lacy things, white powder, and cute-cute-cute
gestures and walks. It might be like a masquerade, but in this case, the
little girl is worn more like a weird flesh or second skin. They may put
on the "girl," but they also transform into the mutant girl. It seems that
at least part of their intention is to offer these leaks in the system of
body reading: confusing age, desire, erotics, and real/artificial per-
ceptions. The result is an incomplete and messy "mutant-cy," their
resemblance of girl-likeness pasted onto mature female bodies. They
leave the audience in discomfort with these ambiguous alternatives: Are
they women doing "girls" for fun? Are they women undoing "girls"?
Are they deliberately eroticising "girls" with their mature female bodies
squeezed into cute acts? And/or who cares if the performance appears
only light and airy? Except, these de-natured girls later strangle each
other, and allow one of them to hang herself while she stuffs her face
with the decaying food of a three-day-old banquet. Double poison?
These de-natured girls raise questions that disturb deeply cherished
notions of innocence and childhood, especially the pretty zone of "little
girl." Yubiwa Hotel explodes the deep mythology of "little girl" using
their alternative methodology of mutation. Thus, their cute mutant girls
offer a scary but seemingly adorable, precious yet obnoxious representation of "girl" consciousness, eros, and trauma.

The de-natured girl roles are not women acting like girls but actually
physically intertwining multiple notions of little girls, cyber girls,
animation girls, fashion girls, and comic girls, into their own version of
"mutant" girls. The mutant girls performance strategies may perform the
"intercorporeal being" that Jones finds in the spectatorial "monstrous"
body found in performance art:

> The particularly identified body/self is always (almost imperceptively) in
> motion, never one with its fantasmagoric projections: with the identities and
> significances that are thrust upon its visible and invisible codes from both
> outside and in. The body/self is reversible (inside/outside are a Möbius-
> strip-like continuum of flesh). The body/self is an "intercorporeal being,"
> fundamentally open to the other. It is the intertwining of self and other (the
> contingency of each on the other – of the "unnatural" on the "natural")...
> (Jones 2000: 15)

Throughout this examination I draw attention to this Möbius-strip-like-continuum of the flesh, where multiple "little girls," women, and other female-like bodies, appear, disappear, and become transparent to each other. Shirotama maintains that she uses the "ordinary" little girl-ness like a symbol but also as something real. She uses the iconicity of girl in Japan, and twists it with the mundane and commercial. Her girls emphasise the profundity of the mundane (or ordinariness of the otherworldly) in their performance of little girl roles and images. The very ordinariness and otherworldliness of the little girl icon speaks to the new century's deepest afflictions and desires.

On the one hand, the little girl image in Japan can maintain a deadly stranglehold on Japanese women if kept rigidly in place and assigned fixed meanings of natural or unnatural. On the other, little girl fluidity and strangeness could force the transformativity of gender, age, and actual physicality, thus, remaking what is generally thought to be universal: the body. The little girl's unnatural acts can shake out the imbedded and entrenched doctrines of opposing and binary female and male genders, bodies, and sexualities. Mimaru, in the *anime Perfect Blue*, is the little girl pop idol who is chased to death by herself, on-screen and off, *existing simultaneously as both* a virtual and real little girl. She cries in her cute girl way when she is dying: "Who is real? What is real?" In *Inori Hataraki*, "live" little girls carry the "dead" little girl, played by Shirotama and place her reverently on to an industrial conveyor belt. The conveyor belt suddenly starts up with a jolt, booming and grinding, her cute pink body messy with chocolate blood, jiggles and bumps along towards the machine's opening. Fondly, the girls watch their sister's "live" body morph. Perhaps the little girl should ask: Who is real? Or better, who is "live"?

Yubiwa Hotel girls squeeze the flesh and cover it with gooey goop; they make girl clothes look like stripper outfits with cute flair. Their extremes borrow from fantasies of violation, abuse, and eroticism. Their dresses are meant to be violated and shredded. Their little girl acts are silly to the point of danger and then some. They do violence to the flesh to attempt to undo the little girl cute. They sink and wallow in conscious girliness. On the contrary, Shirotama says she longs for the pleasure of the curvaceous "Monroe" body to take over the little girl in Japan. She thinks most Japanese women want to remain little girls:

> They long to stay young until they die. They preserve their little girlness. They work at it to the point of dying for it in dieting to fit tiny clothes ... we are also forced to act like little girls to get public attention. (Shirotama 2001)

Shirotama deliberately mutates her little girls with cuteness taken to extremes. Gradually her extremes will transform into alternative visions.

Conclusion

Yubiwa Hotel's "little girls" attempt to dismantle and confuse the codes that bind the female body to pretty, little, and cute-*kawaii*. In my view, the actions of seduction and transformation are crucial to the techniques of these defiant, outrageous, and subtle acts. In these performances the female body is freed from iconic demarcations of female flesh which has bindings and gags on it, in order to become another body that is physical but borrows properties from flesh, fantasy, spirituality, and science: creating cloned and cyborg-like *shôjo* bodies: Mutant Little Girls. In the act of "girling" their bodies, Japanese women usually end up in various positions that are dangerous and ambiguous. In some cases, suicide, continual abuse, death, and self-torture are performed, while in others, the images float away. It is as if the *shôjo* is too much or too "little" for this world and thus escapes censorship, if not death.

Is it possible for Japanese women to put their hyperbolic twist on the hegemonic fashion/commodity industry based on cute to create a potentially transformative space and body? Can they play paradoxical games with visceral and virtual girl archetypes and create a masquerade that can break up a repressive gridlock of approved bodies and behaviours? Is the little girl's song an oracular incantation? I would argue that on one level Japanese women are "deforming" the notion of woman in the Japan with the tools of the commodity culture that are supposed to nurture their sweetness. Too much pink and cuteness makes a deadly "deadly mix" like that found in so many *anime*, where it literally sucks up the space and makes the world, at least in fantasy, a place for divergent, aberrant deviancy that can ignite self-transformative consciousness. Even if it is a mighty romp of dolls and sparkle lights, the festival space of little girl cuteness is a wired space of metamorphosis that defies even the boundaries of transgression. Not only do I think Japanese women can perform different bodies but they also perform Jones's "intercorporeality." I think they must. Or, they will end like the little girl cyborg in the *anime Metropolis* (2000), who performs her little girl heartache by attaching herself to the machine that will destroy the "bad" city. The little girl cyborg is, of course, sacrificed, zapped, and obliterated. She leaves a hole in the universe that is not so far removed from Yubiwa Hotel's dead little girls.

Yubiwa Hotel's unnatural acts of eccentric sweetness, which turn into mutant transformations, signal the little girl's entry into a masquerade, a festival, and techno spirit realm where she can be empowered. "Here" the performer little girls mutate, if only in the moment, into a mix and mess of live and dream-like flesh, sweetness and eroticism, mediatised and spiritualised violence and death. Thus the "Nowhere" girls untie the noose around the dead girl's neck and process out the door singing softly, as the solitary, ghosted singer fades to black on the upper stage pulling back her rope. And thus, the *shôjo* meets her shadow/spirit and flesh and digital embodiment simultaneously and explosively. In her fracturing, the little girl disembodies. Cuteness exceeds the imaginary. Cute mutant girls proliferate. Little girls multiply and morph into alien shapes, creating languages, worlds, and mythologies.

In their performance, their little girl acts becomes transparent with the "live." As I suggested at the beginning, "little girl" performers create a radical coupling and blending of Japanese traditional and contemporary cultural icons. The flesh body melts and reforms into a reversible body in the transient and transcendent space between body and spirit. The mutant little girls make, do and re-form their own bodies into dolls that do not break but can die, regenerate and transform. Yet their mutations require reversibility, which gives them the safety of return: little girls always have a way out, but little girls die too. The game is for very high stakes: altering life on planet Japan may just be in the little girl's reversible realm of mutant-cy. While the little girl on stage is hyperbolising in her pink dress and hairdo, looking too cute, she may be ranting about her desire and longing, not for a past cute innocence, but for her own alien-nation. Her call could be both chant and rant to get out of the cute game. The mutant confusion of Yubiwa Hotel offers an alternative that seduces and repels. The Nowhere girl-chant sweetly recalls the innocent longing of the cute mutant girl heart.

Wandering around the audience and the banquet table, mutant girls chant:

The one you smell,
The one you see,
The one you hear,
The one you touch,
Maybe everything, anything soaks into this "other"[heart]? Or nothing?
Soaking into this "other" [heart]. Everything, anything, nothing? (*Nowhere Girl Episode 2 Poison*, 12. 2002)

Works Cited

Anon. *Bijutsu Techô* 48.720 (1996).
Brehm, Margrit. ed. *The Japanese Experience Inevitable*. Ostfildern-Ruit: Hatje Cantz Verlag, 2002.

Jansen, Gregor. "Yoshimoto Nara Slash with a Small Knife." *The Japanese Experience Inevitable*, ed. Margrit Brehm. Ostfildern-Ruit: Hatje Cantz Verlag, 2002, 136-41.

Jones, Amelia. "Acting Unnatural: Interpreting Body Art." *Decomposition, Post-Disciplinary Performance*, ed. Sue-Ellen Case, Philip Brett, and Susan Leigh Foster. Bloomington: Indiana U. P., 2000.

Morse, Margaret. *Virtualities, Television, Media Art, and Cyberculture.* Bloomington: Indiana U. P., 1998.

Murakami, Takashi. *SUPERFLAT.* Tokyo: Madra Publishing Co, Ltd. 2000.

Napier, Susan J. *Anime, from Akira to Princess Mononoke.* New York: Palgrave, 2000.

Treat, John Whittier. "Yoshimoto Banana Writes Home: The *Shôjo* in Popular Culture." *Contemporary Japan and Popular Culture*, ed. John Whittier Treat. Honolulu: University of Hawai'i Press, 1996, 275-308.

Shirotama Hitsujiya. "Project Plans for Nowhere." *Yubiwa Hotel Profile 2001*, publicity pamphlet. Tokyo: Yubiwa Hotel Front, 2001.

Performances

Yubiwa Hotel. *Muse of Shoes.* Written, directed, and choreographed by Shirotama Hitsujiya. Tokyo, Japan. 1996.

Yubiwa Hotel. *Inori Hataraki.* Written, directed, and choreographed by Shirotama, Hitsujiya. Tokyo, Japan. 2000.

Yubiwa Hotel. *Long Distance Love.* Written, directed and choreographed by Shirotama Hitsujiya. Live Internet Performance. New York, New York, and Tokyo, Japan. 2001.

Yubiwa Hotel. *Nowhere Girl Episode 2 Poison.* Written, directed, and choreographed by Shirotama Hitsujiya Tokyo, Japan. 2002.

Interviews

Shirotama Hitsujiya. Personal Interview. Tokyo, Japan. June 2000.

_____. Personal Interview. Berkeley, CA. October 2001.

_____. Personal Interview. San Francisco, CA. May 2002.

CHAPTER 5

Violence, Corporeality
and Intercultural Theatre

Rachel FENSHAM

> *"Shakespeare invented violence"* WS:HDQ
> *by NYID, 1995.*
>
> *"The practice of violence, like all action,
> changes the world, but the most probable
> change is to a more violent world."* Hannah
> *Arendt,* Crises of the Republic, *1969.*

In the current global context, acts of violence associated with terrorism, conflict and war saturate everyday reality through the representation of bodies bloodied, maimed, beaten or covered in a white sheet. The reality of these acts, as the social theorist Hannah Arendt warns, changes the society in which we live (Arendt 1969: 177). Her collection of essays "on violence" were written at a time when the student uprisings of 1968 in Paris, Berkeley and Tokyo had surprised the Old Left with their willingness to embrace the means of violence. In the aftermath of fascism, the notion of revolution and violent uprising to achieve social change had been largely rejected but a new post-war generation began to reconsider violence as a means of disrupting instruments of state power, such as the police, universities and bureaucracies. At this time, however, the ends of violence were not to take power but to disrupt and change the normal workings of powerful structures and ideologies emerging in the nation-state. Although these essays begin with the need to understand protest movements, they also portend that powers imbued in the concept of the republic, or Western-style participatory democracy, can be turned violently against those which threaten that ideology even if it means denying others the right to live, work, be educated, share resources or have liberty. Since then, systematic yet unpredictable acts of state and religious terrorism have further distorted the relationship between power and violence. Violence, it appears now, is perpetrated by both the doers and receivers of state-sponsored campaigns of repression, intimidation or elimination so that narratives of cause and effect are much more difficult to mount. Indeed, the escalating effects of violence have a hypnotic effect that threatens to render us speechless, as if incapable of critical thought or action. At worst, as Arendt argues, "they put to sleep our common sense," so that the infliction of unwarranted violence, pain or suffering on the body of another is not always seen as an abuse of power (Arendt 1969: 110). But the dehumanisation that accompanies systematic acts of corporeal violence implicates us as its witnesses and makes us responsible for its effects. For Arendt, the counter-activity is critical reason; for contemporary theatre, other acts of creative thinking about violence and its representation are needed.

For theatre artists to contribute to historical consciousness of present social and political conditions, their responsibilities lie in the representation of acts, or the action, of violence. Given the ubiquity of violence in film, on the news and in interactive games, representational violence has today limited connection to political change even though violence and its association with corrupt power was always at the core of tragedy. There has however never been an easy solution for showing violence in the theatre because it tests the border between the virtual and the actual— an actor's body cannot be truly wounded if the performance is to continue. Historically, different strategies have been developed to produce audience consciousness of the emotional and psychological effects of violence without a physical event actually taking place. To avoid the appearance of corpses, battles and murder on stage, ancient Greek theatre deliberately used displacement and reported the most bloody or gruesome acts from the off-stage, or obscene, spaces of the dramatic imagination. In traditional Oriental theatre, the substitution of a red cloth for a stream of blood would follow ritualised gestures such as the slitting of a throat or piercing of a stomach. Modern theatre has relied on the simulation of sound effects and the pretence of bodies being mutilated or collapsing except when the form of torture is encoded in the psychology of language. In more contemporary theatre, the exaggerated theatricalisation of violence is central to the spectacle, such as when groups like La Fura dels Baus threaten the audience with the revving of chainsaws, roaring flames and large projected video images of bloody events.[1] But the attempt to shock through violence has limited uses; although it may produce an immediate histrionic response, the

---

[1]   Their theatre works with the concept of 'transferring radical provocation into an aesthetic form' (Feldman 1999: 34-44).

resulting chaos often diminishes the consequences of violence in a mise en scène. This difficulty of representing violence without replicating its effects has also been a critical problem for twentieth century theatre aesthetics.

Indeed, Artaud and Brecht stand apart on the representation of violence although both insist on the necessary negotiation of the violence of difference. In his mad vision, Artaud regarded the cruelty of the viscera, literally the guts of the human being, and its intensification on stage as a means of animating the corpse, of seeing the violence done to bodies by objects and forces external to the self. Brecht, on the other hand, wanted to stand back from violence in order to observe the dialectic through which violence in the individual is complicit with the forces of power in modern society. More recent postmodern theatre has tried to combine the social significance of Brechtian aesthetics with an Artaudian immersion in subjectivity by translating the immediacy and social disturbance of violence through the corporeality of its actors. Elin Diamond writes of a theatre in which the "sentient knowledge of a body's otherness" conditions the performance so that spectators experience suffering, pain, joy or anguish as the subjective dimensions of a social and cultural materiality (Diamond 1995: 161). Violence imagined through performance can therefore produce a felt objectivity towards the corporeal conditions which constitute the specific otherness of a given reality. In this way, to witness the appearance of bodies "mobilised and annihilated by discourse" as if in a state of "permanent catharsis," has been a deliberate strategy of postmodern theatre to make corporeal violence visible as a means and ends of power (Diamond 1995: 167). Theatre has thus moved towards the actualisation of violence as corporeal rather than avoiding its bodily effects through the virtuality of representation.

Whatever the varied success of physical, visual or spectacular theatre, I want to suggest in this paper, following Arendt, that corporeal violence must also be linked to a concept of action. In recent performance theory, notions of action have often been identified with the exhausted motivations of realist bourgeois theatre but it may be important to retrieve its political expediency and creative value. In an action someone does something to someone that changes a situation. An action whether public or private can also be shown and seen. An action has agency, and does not have to be explained by theories of causation, which would attribute accountability, or blame, to an individual or representative history. Understanding action as causality itself means trying to understand how something happens and not why. Action, according to Arendt, is a primary function and faculty of human beings and she suggests that the action of violence works in conjunction with the nature and use of power (1969: 179; 142-155). In this essay, I rework her ideas about violence and action in relation to the theatrical use of violence although I am aware that her intention was more pragmatically an attempt to explain the operations of power in a post-war reality. Her ideas however provide a starting point from which to construct some reflections on the responsibility, creative and critical, of contemporary artists and audiences towards the body witnessed as a corporeal limit of the human being.

I will consider how an Australian theatre company, Not Yet It's Difficult (NYID), has negotiated through representation the human capacity to dehumanise or annihilate others. My focus will be on the corporeality, what Susan Foster calls the "physicality of meaning-making," that occurs in theatre performance (Foster 1996: xiii). NYID is a Melbourne-based performance company that utilises a variety of deconstructive performance techniques to examine contemporary culture. Although violence is not their subject matter, its productions engage in a Foucauldian way with political issues, examining in particular the material effects of discourse on the body of the actor.[2] In this sense, they remain concerned with textuality, since language and the formal codification of gesture are primary mediators of their performances. Since 1999 they have collaborated with Japanese theatre company Gekidan Kaitaisha in a long-term intercultural project that culminated in a final production called *Journey to Con-Fusion 3* in 2002. Although the two companies have different histories and different aesthetics, they share a critical and dystopian view of postmodern culture and its effects upon the human subject. These NYID projects suggest a range of approaches to violence as embodied action in contemporary theatre.

The Sword, the Stick, the Slap, the Knife, the Razor Blade, the Suicide Bomb

Arendt repeatedly states that violence is instrumental and requires implements to increase and multiply human strength. Phenomeno-logically, the violence of weapons is aligned to corporeal strength until the weapons become its substitute (Arendt 1969: 145). In other words, the implements of violence are real objects that enhance a body until they exceed and overpower its autonomy. The danger of a weapon is

---

[2]   I am referring here to Foucault's analysis of the disciplinary convergence between power and knowledge (Foucault 1977).

however the power to which it is attached and the obedience to its conditions, usually fatal, that is required as a response. Only heroes argue with a loaded gun. As Arendt cautions, power dominates violence (Arendt 1969: 151). There are many implements of violence, including on my list, the sword, the stick, the slap, the knife, the razor blade or the suicide bomb. We improvise our weapons according to our means except in the strategic theatre of state warfare. In theatre, weapons are often used as implements for the display of power or the dramatic re-enactment of conflict. Weapons of destruction become semiotically, what Lesley Stern calls "supercharged objects, almost magical in their effects" on stage; since they appear to do violence without human agency. Rather than attach violent instruments to character, it is the objects themselves that produce an excess of signification – "excessive desire, ambition, pleasure, colour, speed" – from which the articulation of a specific energy comes (Stern 1995: 266).

An illustration of the energetic potency of the weapon occurs in *WS: HDQ* (*William Shakespeare: Hung Drawn and Quartered*), a performance in which NYID ritually destroy Shakespeare's textual authority. An actor's announcement that "Shakespeare invented violence" is deliberately provocative about the power of his world over many colonial subjects. Indeed, Shakespeare provides an "ur-text" of battles, fights and individually destructive acts that justify historical wars as well as model other forms of social conflict. Performing the spectacle of violence in Shakespeare requires the use of weaponry for sport and murder as well as an enhanced physicality. Following a list of Shakespeare's many "inventions," a choreographed fight scene between Paul Bongiovanni and Kha Tran Viet takes place in which they display skills in the martial arts of sword, stick and kick-fighting. On the proscenium stage, the performance presents as showmanship, a chance for celebrating each individual combatant within defined rules and codes of conduct. When one performer escapes only to reappear in the open space between the audience, this becomes the arena for a more intense conflict between two parties. The swords flash in their hands, skewering one against a wall, flicking and cutting across the other, then pressing steel on steel against the floor. Then their sticks crash and bang, ending in a defensive crossed position that can only be broken by the return of the swords. With more vivid leaps and turns, the two mock warriors slide across the floor, at once foiled in the act of maiming each other. The trope of the fight can be seen here to work in two ways: on the one hand, it is utterly predictable because it has no apparent object, its beguiling function is the theatrical repetition of violence so that the audience takes pleasure only in its dynamic energy. On the other, the representation glorifies the warrior, whose strength and resilience becomes visible as a fictional supplement to the body of the actor. Thus, the weapon reproduces the appearance of an heroic power in which violence is an imaginary potential of male bodies condoned in the familiar action of conflict. In the NYID performance however the violence of a classic fight scene both exceeds and isolates its power from historical figures, giving it only the energy of play within the corporeality of those who are its temporary instrument.

By way of contrast, the intense repetitive slapping of Kumamoto Kenjiro from the Kaitaisha company in their performance of *Tokyo Ghetto* is effected at a level of actuality on the skin. He hits first a woman's back and finally for an intolerably long time his own knees until his flesh reddens and he drops to the ground. According to Peter Eckersall, this surface inscription of the body "is designed to draw attention to how authoritarian and monolithic forms of enculturation might work in Japanese society" (Eckersall 2001: 312-328). The complicity of the actors with this action draws attention to a corporeality that is the instrumentality of violence and not its object. The cultural contrast is worth noting since the Japanese male body has less recourse to glorified images of warrior violence since the humiliating defeat of World War Two, and therefore the self-inflicted weaponry of the slap serves a different referential function. It achingly defends a public subjectification that is starkly opposed to the affirmation of the sword, chivalry and victory identified with Shakespeare. Both instruments however serve the agency of patriarchal power, as Stern observes, "partly because the energies (both ecstatic and destructive) unleashed ... are invested ... via these objects or tropes" (Stern 1995: 266).

Later in *WS:HDQ*, instrumental violence manifests less directly when the "book" is used as a psychological weapon able to destroy the actor who says "to be or not to be" incorrectly. Judith Butler's (1990) critique of performative language notes that failure to perform the linguistic injunctions of dominant discourse is punishable and in this performance, the punishment is physically effected. Every time the acting teacher played by Maude Davey insists that Greg Ulfan has got the rhythms of Shakespeare's speech wrong, he is slapped across the back and legs with the *Complete Works*. An implicit violence in theatre is thus made visible as the practice of an imperial textual authority whose ideological reproduction of proper or legitimated English has maimed thousands of actors, forcing them to repeat its codified rules and reiterate its battles. In this sense, the instrumentality of theatre as another mode of doing violence is also deconstructed by NYID. This interrogation of the weapons of theatrical discourse provides them with a means in subsequent productions of decoding other powerful mediated structures.

Power, Mass Formation and Violence

For Arendt, there are many differences between power and violence. Power is not violence, indeed "everything depends on the power behind the violence" (Arendt 1969: 148). Violence can in fact produce effects without power because its instrumentality is a force that can destroy without justification. Power, on the other hand, has legitimacy given to it by a collective of people, usually in the past, whose continuing endorsement determines the structure and values of social formations (Arendt 1969: 140). Power attached to violence is thus legitimated by concepts of justice. Violence can never be legitimate in any rational sense, even though it might be justified in terms of an immediate future where the ends can effect a swift outcome (Arendt 1969: 151). The question of whether violence is ever justified has been intensively debated in the light of European fascism that many regarded as an evil to be stopped by violent means rather than peaceful negotiation. Arendt considers the possibility that violence might be justified in certain circumstances where it is the "only way to set the scales of justice right again" (Arendt 1969: 161) although she never gives it reason. Without entering here into a discussion of whose scales and what the "only way" might mean, the notion of a violence that might intervene in circumstance "when our sense of justice is offended" is potent for theatre practice (Arendt 1969: 160).

The violence of corporate fascism concerned NYID in their performance of the *Melbourne Festival Training Squad*, an outdoor program of the Melbourne Festival in 1997. In this work, a squadron of nine hyper-fit actors ran, jumped and shouted their way around Melbourne's city streets in a parody of the training programs and heroic displays that sportsmen ritually and routinely present in Australian culture. At intervals the lycra-and-labelled "team" would stop and demonstrate on a whistle blow, their strength and agility in a range of active sports – boxing, football, martial arts, body-building. Slogans about the consumption of art, the obsession with power, the dominance of the physical were shouted and projected over them. In this performance, the massed bodies of contest converged hypnotically with the power of corporate culture and the localised effects of a state leader's self-aggrandisement through major sporting events. From one critic's perspective, NYID's representational strategy reproduced a traditional image of fascism: "The content never shifted from being acquisitive, and ultimately became a militaristic self-glorification. Some kind of irony or an unexpected dissolving of power could have been created if the work had ... a failure of some kind, or complete megalomania" (Connors 1996/7: 33). In this example, the allegiance of the actors to the performance of certain actions under orders deliberately, if confrontingly, threatened to replicate the violence of a mass formation.

In Arendt's terms, dangerous revolutionary or military action occurs when obedience to the group legitimates a particular form of power without allowing individual or democratic dissent and when the group's immortality "is actualised in the practice of violence" (Arendt 1969: 165). If a power structure remains fully in control only through the ongoing use of violence, then the possibility of terrorism emerges. On the street, the NYID actors represented a powerful machine-like body politic through a sleek physicality identified with the legitimate actions of corporate culture. But its ironic display was further evidence that this form of power is effective only through the endorsement of its public. Most spectators watching this event were both seduced and appalled by the mesmerising qualities of the disciplined mass of bodies but could also hear the corrupted slogans that operated as a counter-offensive to expose, rather than condone, totalitarian power used as public spectacle. Since the alignment of bodies with ideology was made explicit rather than left unnamed, the performance was an intervention that subversively parodied rather than mimicked the coercive operations of government propaganda.

This same squadron-like running was critically different in a later visit of NYID to Tokyo in which Kaitaisha joined them in performing "the Cube." As an action, it produced an alternative meditation on the power of social structures. As Ed Scheer notes "the performers ... run in formation through the streets of Tokyo. More than simply training it ironically recasts sports training in a performance situation. This combination of a rigorous shape in a shapeless environment, a formal jog through the city, reframes the city in human terms. The reordering also occurs in the unstructured moments of the performance itself and suggests a way of thinking about this project ... as a redistribution of the notion of the formless" (2001: 83-4). Scheer observes in the rigorous pattern of movement that the articulation of a different sense of bodies can be attributed to its performative function and not to an overt ideological content. The group by now comprised varying physiological and cultural differences across ages, genders, nationalities and their collective running provided them with a rhythmical alternative to social order. The idea that violent acts can have an "antipolitical character ... does not mean that they are inhuman or 'merely' emotional" (Arendt 1969: 161). Nor does a violent action performed without question by performers have to be the product of objectified power because it might also estrange individuals from their co-option to other totalities or collective identities. In what Scheer calls the "formlessness" of diverse corporealities within the structure, that is, actors from two companies unused to working together, a different politics begins to appear. The violence of differently gendered and racialised bodies given temporary unity through the power of movement became also a violence of estrangement that could insert itself non-violently inside other structures of power. This theatre formation suggests a model of civil action that can intervene against violence that claims to be legitimate without being just. Before discussing further this idea of an alternative civility in the NYID/Kaitaisha intercultural exchange, it is pertinent to reflect further upon another project in which NYID significantly examine the violence of racism in Australian culture.

Racism, Rhetoric and Catharsis

Arendt describes the extreme form of power as "All Against One," the extreme form of violence as "One against All" (Arendt 1969: 141). As she notes, there is a logic that has operated many times over, that a social group remains unified, through division, by isolating its victims. NYID's production of the *Austral/Asian Post-Cartoon: Sports Edition* presented in 1997 deconstructed anti-Asian discourses then circulating in Australia under the influence of Pauline Hanson's One Nation Party.[3] NYID linked political rhetoric operating in the language of sport with physical action in order to illustrate well-established connections between concepts of nationalism and racial intolerance. The violence of sport thus facilitated a dramatic representation of the "new racism" in which beliefs are "not based on biological superiority but on the incompatibility of cultural traditions" (Stratton 1998: 62). In the discourse of a dominant white Australian culture, beliefs in a superior corporeality of some and not others is codified and coordinated by capitalist and nationalist interests. How words produce racism in the movement from language to physical action, or in the slippage from the All to the One, can be made visible in performance.

One particular scene constructed by NYID in consultation with Australian Vietnamese actor Kha replicated an interracial fight by mimicking the competitive ethos of two rival sporting teams. The energised pep-talk from the coach, played by director David Pledger, emphasised the need to vanquish one's opponents but also interpellated

---

[3]   A longer analysis of this performance appeared in Fensham 2000.

an object of the group's disgust – the body which does not belong to Australian culture, the young Asian male.[4] Once warmed up, the coach called for someone to strike the outsider down – "who will strike? Who will strike?"[5] The sense of collective hatred became palpable but eventually someone from within the group moved – they must, as they had been prepared to take action without reason. And the insults became beatings, kicks and shouting. For a while, Kha stood his ground, he was wearing a protective vest, but was eventually cast down with a thunderous slamming of sticks. There was a man on the ground beaten by many who acted without consciousness of this body's humanity.

The audience witnessed this brutal destructiveness as an unleashed, unreasonable violence. The scene was extremely disturbing, someone let out a cry and people were numbed by what they had seen. Later, some audience members were angry with the excessive re-enactment of racial violence. This action effectively brought the audience towards a repre-sentational crisis. It raised the question of how to look, or not to look, at a racial violence that dehumanises bodies, whether in the staging of tragedy or in the televisual representation of war crimes. Although the performance operated with sufficient theatricality to suggest that the attack was not real, it ineluctably pointed towards a correlative social outcome from racist discourse. Shocked into silence, the audience confronted the possibility of racism as an action which scars and kills. As Arendt writes "the logical and rational consequence of ... an explicit ideological system" such as racism, is a violence that is "always murder-ous" (Arendt 1969: 173). This realisation is particularly unsettling to a theatre audience isolated by bourgeois habits from racial violence in the streets.

Audience discomfort was vociferously expressed in disagreement about the gratuity or appropriateness of allowing this other body to carry the burden of victim. But what was at stake was another question: why and how does a critical rupture in "structures of feeling" – through the double process of identification and disidentification with another's body – produce the affect of horror? And how can we respond? In this performance, the irrationality of revulsion towards another had been rendered linguistic, visual and physical through a structured sequence of actions. Diamond's notion of a "shuddering without end" seems jus-tified by this event, since embodiment had intensified the closeness

---

4   White Australia has a long history of animosity towards Asia, and for many years it
      was official policy to exclude Asians from immigration.
5   Transcribed copy of NYID script.

between the representational and the real by insisting on the immediacy of corporeal violence. The extremity of this All against One event produced apprehension without comprehension. Dramaturgically, another action, perhaps of a different catharsis, was needed if the power of acceding to violence through silent witness of the One was to be rejected.

Dehumanisation, Interruption and Violence

Arendt argues that violence is not an irrational act, because that claim would diminish human responsibility for action (Arendt 1969: 160). If, for instance, apparently democratic public institutions no longer serve people, an act of violence that stops their inhumanity may be an appropriate action. Or, it may be necessary to interrupt the idea of progress, an ideology endorsed by state powers to uphold their rights to govern, colonise and command obedience, through violent means. "If this were true, if only the practice of violence would make it possible to interrupt automatic processes in the realm of human affairs, the preachers of violence would have won an important point" (Arendt 1969: 132). Without violence, however, acts of interruption are potent critical tools for asking structures of power and systems of belief to account for their use of violence or destruction. It is the function of all action, she continues, "to interrupt what otherwise would have proceeded automatically and therefore predictably" (Arendt 1969: 133). Interruption thus enables a break in the concept of history, of the forward flow of time, of the sequential nature of events, for critical reflection and response.

Given the combination of instantaneous media coverage and the relentless mechanisms of international law in providing an analysis of violent global events, it is often difficult to know how to interrupt the flow of information. And it is even more difficult with reason to hold one person or group accountable for specific violent actions without being caught up in the forward movement through which conflicting ideas, actions and peoples are realigned by social forces. In critical theory, the concept of interruption has had validity as an aesthetic response to textual closure, as for instance when an image or word arrests the attention of a spectator or reader so that we are forced to reconsideration of a work of art. The interruption of time, the tearing away at the structure of a text or the splitting open of idealised relations between image and identity have thus been key functions of artistic practice in the twentieth century. For this reason, images of violence and dehumanisation, as I have argued, are not without means in the theatre. But the potential of action to interrupt performance, especially at the height of its intensity, in order to stop the ongoing flow of signification is equally as important.

In the NYID performance, the violence of the bashing scene in the *Sports Edition* critically stopped the anonymity of racism through the specificity of Kha's corporeality. If team sport was synecdoche for nationalism, the unifying power of the One, it was his "non-sporting body" that was metonymic of the hated other. But his "sporting body" apparently immobilised by the violent outcomes of racial discourse also interrupted the inevitability of this progression through the All. So that the "corpse" could no longer represent a finite reference point, he stood up and spoke back to the other actors. He invited them to strike him again in order for him to teach them how to fight according to a different set of rules, those of the Vietnamese martial art Vovinam. In combination with quick and clever gestures, his words instructed them to show respect for the opponent, to play with deflection and retreat as much as attack, and within three moves, the audience was laughing at their previous disturbance. As an actor he moved in this action from the representational to the presentational, becoming himself, the young Asian man teaching the white audience to negotiate his difference. His cultural autonomy was enhanced through this physical prowess in ways that contrasted sharply with the irrational obedience to physical contest of his attackers. This theatrical act of intra-culturalism, a between-cultures exchange of modes of practice, was also a symbolic gift of conciliation towards the indifference that governs the formation of social attitudes within the nation-state. Interruption thus became a necessary mechanism for a catharsis that could overturn powerful norms regulating embodied cultural difference. This example suggests that theatre can interrupt the mechanisms and effects of violence, whether in rhetoric or action, in order to further our capacity to recognise how power is internalised and used to enforce the values of a particular regime.

Intercultural Theatre and Violence

In the political and artistic practices of this already battle-scarred twenty-first century, different modes of thinking about the cultural violence done to bodies are needed. While post-structuralism has made us suspicious of totalising theories of the body, it has also alerted us to the difficulty of maintaining an uncritical assessment of the human. But a writer such as Arendt reminds us also that we cannot ignore inhumanity, the continuation of war and the difficult negotiation of just compromises. In the experiments of avant garde theatre companies, there have been many elusive promises about theatres relationship to social change but it is often in the corporeality of its practices that new insights appear. On a micro-level, many global concerns about violence are investigated, I would contend, daily, hourly, weekly, annually by artists and their audiences, particularly in the context of intercultural theatre.

In the Australia-Japan collaboration between NYID and Kaitaisha, the dialectic within Western modernity of the Artaud-Brecht distinction has been replaced by a commitment to an aesthetics of interruption, to the performance of actions that violate cultural certainties through work on the body. Each company is constituted by different conceptions of the political peculiar to their own country and to their own theoretical stance: NYID engages more directly with social commentary while Kaitaisha is more concerned with social alienation. In their four year exchange project, both directors have however identified the semiotics of power as a fundamental question for contemporary theatre. And they are both critically attuned to the ways in which image, language, bodies and movement produce violence, even though their directorial approaches to its representation are radically different.[6]

Kaitaisha director Shimizu Shinjin demands from his actors allegiance to a theatre based on intensive physical training and amplification of the effects of power in visual, sound and physical action. Through the externalisation of internal actions in the nervous system, a disturbed and fragmented appearance of the body mediates images of violence that seem transhistorical. Shimizu instructs his actors "to not focus, just keep twitching, you are always under surveillance." Subject to a postmodern condition associated by both Fukuyama and Baudrillard with the ends of history, the body of a Kaitaisha actor thus oscillates like a surface transmitter rather than a means of transcendence. Bodies appear to be fully colonised by power and can be used theatrically as receptors or relays for many different kinds of violence. In the total spectacle, video-art, sound, lighting etc. provide intertextual references to war, defoliated landscapes and sexual violence but they also represent the mechanisms for dissemination of power and provide the means for corporeal interaction with technologies of power. By way of contrast, David Pledger, the NYID director, commands authority over his actors but also requires their mutual involvement in a theatre that can name and test the legitimacy of power. His use of a gestural choreography to signify the instrumentality of violence aims to make visible how systems of control or political manipulation are constructed. The banality of indoctrination is

---

[6] I participated in a Tokyo symposium during stage two of this collaboration in which the directors of both companies answered questions about their work from actors, theatre critics and scholars. Further discussion of that project and the intercultural issues of this theatre exchange can be found in Eckersall *et al.* 2001.

rendered through an excessive or sordid repetition of physical action, with the exteriority of the body as exemplary model. Perhaps the permanent contradiction of NYID is that corporeality – bound, trussed and violent – remains a critical source of inspiration for political action through the theatre. And in that sense, resistant bodies that continue to interrupt these powerful social and dramatic formations are also critical actors.

Both these directors, historically and culturally marked, therefore attempt to negotiate difficult conditions within violence for the representation of power. In the final exchange performance of *Journey to Con-Fusion*, it is both the incommensurability of these different approaches and the shared attempt to give explicit form to violence in the body that is illuminating. A jerky duet danced by both the Japanese and Australian performers is interrupted by the sound and sudden appearance of a man throwing another man against the wall over and over. This aesthetics of violence allows for an interruption that functions, and is most effective, when it not only displays but disrupts hegemonic conceptions of national cultures, and their apparent unity or disunity, as well as their means of producing specific corporealities. It also intercedes in the difficult dance of intercultural exchange under tense global conditions. The ambivalence of each actor, whatever their nationality or training, towards these different modes of embodiment, ever so partially exposed the very difficulty of seeing an alternative to the violence erected by different political systems or by and between different cultural groups.

Conclusion

In this essay, I have tried to examine some of the creative actions undertaken between NYID and Kaitaisha in their negotiation of contemporary political violence. These theatrical actions range from display of its weapons to the making of a shared collective estrangement, from apprehension of its corporeal effects to interruption of the mechanisms of power behind violence. Arendt is critical of the equation between creativity and violence, for her there is no philosophical or political justification for the naturalising of violence as a creative act. It is only action that can stand against violence misused by power and it is that action that remains creative:

> What makes man (*sic*) a political being is his faculty of action; it enables him to get together with his peers, to act in concert, and to reach out for goals and enterprises that would never enter his mind, let alone the desires of his heart, had he not being given this gift – to embark on something new (Arendt 1969: 179).

Acting in concert towards something new is what engages intercultural theatre practitioners. During rehearsals for *Journey to Con-Fusion*, the final stage of the NYID/Kaitaisha project in 2002, Pledger took the combined company of actors through a workshop exercise called "Body Listening."[7] It required concentrated group movement in which the actors are clusters of dispersed bodies alternately stopping and walking forward. Each cluster has a unified force determined kinesthetically with the result that some groups stay together surging forward while others become fragmented and widely distributed. Pledger describes this as "diasporic" movement, a greatly simplified image of massive population flows. What is significant however is that the image he gives them in order to remain connected to one another is that of the body as an ear. Instead of representing the human body as willed forward by its head (Western) or by its centre (Eastern), this image suggests the whole surface of the skin becomes a fleshy receptor towards others. If performance is a form of cultural rehearsal for action, this corporeality of listening may be a means for negotiating the infinite violence possible when persons of different social and political histories must co-exist. Although we struggle to justify corporeal violence in contemporary theatre it is also a place to practice and to imagine in the most limited and minute of circumstances – creative, political, social – the action of bodies needed for the continued commitment to what Arendt calls a civil society.

Works Cited

Arendt, H. "On Violence." *Crises of the Republic.* New York: Harcourt Brace Jovanovich, 1969: 105-198.

Butler, J. *Gender Trouble: Feminism and the Subversion of Identity.* London: Routledge, 1990.

Connors, C. "Street Theatre Seriously." *RealTime* 16, December-January 1996/7: 33.

Diamond, E. "The Shudder of Catharsis in Twentieth Century Performance." *Performativity and Performance*, eds. Andrew Parker & Eve Kosofsky Sedgwick. London: Routledge, 1995: 152-172.

Eckersall, P. "The Performing Body and Cultural Representation in the Theatre of Gekidan Kaitaisha." *Japanese Theatre and the International Stage*, eds. Stancia Scholz-Cionca, Samuel Leiter. Leiden: Brill, 2001: 312-328.

Eckersall, P., Fensham, R., Scheer, E., Varney, D. "Tokyo Diary." *Performance Research*, Vol. 6, No. 1, 2001: 71-86.

---

[7] Personal observation of rehearsal process, Melbourne, May 2002.

Feldman, S. G. "Faust in Barcelona, Catalonia's La Fura dels Baus." *Theatre Forum*, No. 15, Summer/Fall, 1999: 34-44.

Fensham, R. "Anti-Asian Rhetoric in Performance." Alter/Asians: Asian-*Australian Identities in Art, Media and Popular Culture*, eds. Ien Ang, Sharon Chalmers, Lisa Law, Mandy Thomas. Sydney: Pluto Press, 2000: 169-182.

Foster, S. L. ed. *Corporealities: Dancing Knowledge, Culture and Power.* London: Routledge, 1996.

Foucault, M. *Discipline and Punish: The Birth of the Prison.* London: Penguin, 1977

Stern, L. "Meditation on Violence." *Kiss Me Deadly: Feminism and Cinema for the Moment*, ed. Laleen Jayamanne. Sydney: Power Institute of Fine Arts, 1995: 252-285.

Stratton, J. *Race Daze: Australia in Identity Crisis.* Sydney: Pluto Press, 1998.

CHAPTER 6

A Phantom of Suburbia:
Kawamura Takeshi's *Hamletclone*

MORIYAMA Naoto

My purpose in this essay is to consider a particular body image that has characterised many of the Japanese contemporary theatres in the 1990s. I will do this task through the analysis of *Hamletclone* (first performed in 2000), a recent work by Kawamura Takeshi and his company Daisan Erotica.[1] From the title we can see that the word "clone" is closely related to the question of body image. The reason why Kawamura has become interested in this question seems clear: as has been mentioned on many occasions, one of the central concerns of Kawamura as an artist and his subsequent privileging of a clone-like body image in his theatre has been the influence of the body of the tragic cyborg characters in the famous Hollywood film *Blade Runner* (Ridley Scott 1982). Unlike human beings, the clone body is similar to the cyborg in that it is directly created from an artificial process and, therefore, lacks its own personal history. As we shall see questions of self identity and the status of the body in contemporary Japanese society are central themes in Kawamura's theatrical and political outlook.

Additionally, there is another body image that constitutes a significant part of this play; that is the body of the phantom. Needless to say, this type of body image has much to do with Shakespeare's *Hamlet*, a source text for *Hamletclone* (alongside Heiner Müller's play

---

[1] Strictly speaking, the name *Hamletclone* has two different meanings here. First, it is the title of the recent work by Kawamura Takeshi that was staged in Tokyo, Osaka, and Nagoya in January 2000. On the other hand, it also indicates a one-year-long project including some workshops and work-in-progress performances staged in August 1999. As for the performance script of *Hamletclone*, the text of the 2000 version and that of 1999 are considerably different from each other. Although both of them are available in Japanese, for the purpose of this essay I will exclusively treat the 2000 version by the name of *Hamletclone*. In my opinion, it contains many more aspects from which we can see what Kawamura tries to do more clearly.

Hamletmachine of which more will said below). In responding to both we might say that *Hamletclone* is a good example of intertextuality in which the idea of the original is questioned and then applied in some different social and theatrical contexts. Identifying and discussing the significance of these moments of intertextuality in *Hamletclone* is one of the aims of the present essay.

Scholars have already addressed some of the general trends and themes in Daisan Erotica's theatre (see Eckersall 2000, Uchino 2000), noting that it has been twenty years since Kawamura began his career as a playwright, a director, and sometimes actor. In the early 1980s, both he and his company were among the central figures of Japan's burgeoning "new theatre" movement that was shifting from a more underground "small theatre" phase to one that was gaining wider popularity and acceptance. This development, during the 1980s bubble economy era in Japan, has been called the "small theatre boom" (see Senda 1988). Unlike other theatre groups of the era, Daisan Erotica has always cut an oppositional profile and has tried to make theatrical statements that critically oppose existing social conditions of Japan. One such target has been the rapidly growing consumer society. As I limit myself to consideration of only one of Kawamura's latest works, this essay does not intend to advance some comprehensive theory about Kawamura's attitude towards theatre and politics, nor the Japanese society at large. However, it should also be noted that the social and theatrical are inseparable in Kawamura's work. As *Hamletclone* addresses many of the problems that Japanese society has been confronting in recent times we gain insight into Japan's social condition. In this essay I will discuss what kind of problems Kawamura is concerned with in *Hamletclone* and how these relate to questions of politics, authority and power among the majority, mainstream, middle class, suburban, affluent Japanese people. I will consider how *Hamletclone* is a critique of power in Japan that sees a return of certain forms of authoritarianism to the Japanese landscape, and as a mindset among Japanese people.

As mentioned above, *Hamletclone* is based on two preceding works: Shakespeare's *Hamlet* and Müller's *Hamletmachine*. Kawamura has been concerned with these artists for more than 10 years. Thus, he made two adaptations of Shakespeare's plays in the early 1990s: *A Man Named Macbeth* (first performed in 1990), and *The Butcher of Titus* (first performed in 1993). He also read *Hamletmachine* for the first time in 1992 when the first Japanese translation was published.[2] Kawamura was greatly impressed by this extremely short, supposedly enigmatic verbal text and was eager to make his own response to Müller's work that drew on his own situation as an artist. We can say that the continuous references to Shakespeare in *Hamletmachine* alongside Müller's challenge to Shakespeare have had a clear and decisive influence on the wider activities of Kawamura and have enabled him to move into a new phase of writing and directing.

***

The drama *Hamletclone* consists of ten scenes. It takes the form of an autobiography; all of the scenes are framed by a narrative commentary delivered by a character called the Old Gay Prince, who is imprisoned in a tower somewhere. Kawamura performs the Gay Prince himself, speaking the lines through a microphone while seated on a platform behind the audience and dressed in "faux Shakespeare" tights and russets.

The characterisation of the Gay Prince is quite complicated; first the Prince tells us that he was imprisoned because he was gay – or more correctly became gay at some stage of his princely life and was subsequently imprisoned. He further tells us that he decided to become gay because he wanted to give up the role of Prince Hamlet in order to play/become Ophelia. This situation compares with the first-person narrator of *Hamletmachine*. The subsequent message of confused sexuality has made the Prince anathema to most people; while at the same time others secretly adore him and want to "reform" their country with him as leader. Although the Prince was steadfastly disinclined to participate in real politics, he has repeatedly been forced to get involved in such intrigues. In order to escape from his "reformer" supporters, he sometimes declares that he became gay, and sometimes declares he became woman (Ophelia). Further complicating matters is the addition of three more actors performing the role of the Prince in his youth. The first performs the male Prince, the second the gay Prince – crossed dressed for the occasion – and the third the female Prince.

At the beginning of the performance of *Hamletclone*, the audience is immediately confronted by the confined theatrical space. When the audience comes into the theatre they find themselves standing on the stage looking through a barbed wire fence at the auditorium. Armed guards patrol to keep people away from their seats that are visible on the other

---

[2]   Translated into Japanese by Iwabuchi Tatsuji and Tanigawa Michiko and published by Miraisha, Tokyo, 1992.

side of the wire. The audience is forced to wait for some time; meanwhile costumed waiters bring them drinks. Behind are two large projection screens on which psychedelically processed images of the Japanese national flag (*Hinomaru*) are incessantly projected. The effect is such that the audience might feel as if they were invited to a banquet hosted by some rich right-wing politician or activist. In this play, we are supposed to be the private guests of the Gay Prince who is going to talk about his life. The reference to neo-nationalism is reinforced when a man on a bicycle comes into the acting space and begins to move through the audience while singing the Japanese national anthem (*Kimigayo*). He grumbles:

> You're asking me who I am? Who do you think you are? If either of us gives our name the civil war will begin.... Myself demanding civil war, I demand to play Hamlet. (Kawamura 2000a)

Guards come and block him, knocking him to the ground. As soon as he falls electric music blasts out at full volume. At this moment, standing in the auditorium, all the characters of *Hamletclone* appear like ghosts, their bodies quivering convulsively.

After this impressive prologue, the Prince gives his permission for the audience to take their seats. Then on the stage we view a series of devastating sights and images of the today's Tokyo.

The scene following the prologue is about the disruption of family. The man who rode the bicycle in the first scene is now called "the Thief." He is in despair at his family. His wife and children are entirely indifferent to each other – a typical image of recent family problems in Japan. In order to restore some sense of unity to his family, the Thief attempts to make them perform the play *Hamlet* because he thinks it is a play about regular family life. As if playing some kind of "drama therapy," the thief casts his family in the roles of Shakespeare's tragedy; his wife is cast as Gertrude, his three sons as Claudius, Polonius, and Horatio, his daughter as Ophelia, and the Thief himself as Prince Hamlet. However, this attempt to renew the family results in failure. When he gives them the lines, they refuse to speak them. Instead the words that come from their mouths are the words of *Hamletmachine*. The Thief flies into a fury and kills all of his family with a baseball bat. A picture of destitution, he then wanders from the house, and joins the crowded chaos of the streets outside. The family members soon revive as if nothing has happened. They also run away, in all directions – like ghosts who rise from their graves and fly into the city. The family then take part in another story, the story of revolution in which the Gay Prince will become involved.

At this point in the play the Thief is homeless. The son whom the Thief once cast as Horatio is engineering a plot to stage a *coup d'état* with a young neo-fascist. Instead of being a philosopher, Horatio is now a nihilistic pornographic-video maker. He is experiencing doubts about the feasibility of his plans. The son who was cast as Polonius is committing adultery with the woman once cast as Gertrude, whereas Laertes works in a gay club passing time together with the Gay Prince. Eventually, Horatio's *coup d'état* proves unsuccessful, the young neo-fascist commits *harakiri* (ritual disembowelment) in a manner reminiscent of Mishima Yukio (who sensationally committed ritual suicide following his own unsuccessful coup in 1970). Polonius, Claudius and Gertrude kill one another in a duel. Since these scenes are often performed in a highly caricatured manner – for example, one is performed through imitating motions of the *Bunraku* puppet theatre – they look more like farce than satire and again nobody dies in a realistic manner.

Meanwhile there is another group trying to carry out their own revolution. The daughter (once cast as Ophelia) joins the Stalk Party, a secret society of battered women who finally succeed in establishing a new government. The Thief participates in the women's uprising and is promoted to the role of Cabinet Minister in the new government. Their reign is short lived, however, and at the end of this play everything disappears, except for the Thief who is left alone. Firing guns into the air he shouts:

> Don't think I am a fool. No more am I a cheap thief. I am the Minister. I have become a great man. (Kawamura 2000a)

Everything that has happened until now reads like a daydream of the Thief, or maybe of the Gay Prince. From another perspective, everything looks like the collective nightmare of the audience, with Kawamura's Prince – as a psychoanalyst – sitting behind the audience listening to their fevered dreams. Projected images, such as historical photos of Japanese soldiers and the mushroom cloud of the A bomb, are metaphorically inserted between the scenes of *Hamletclone* to evoke the collective national memories of war among the audience.

***

As mentioned above, Kawamura begins *Hamletclone* with a narrative about the disruption of the family. What Kawamura tries to show is that the meaning of family in Japan has come to be understood (or more correctly exposed in Kawamura's piece) as an historical product associated with the high growth period of the Japanese economy (1960-89). We might note that this is also the period when Kawamura himself was brought up. One of the central points of interest in *Hamletclone* is the way that Hamlet, as a drama of a royal family, becomes a "double" of nuclear families living in the modern commuter suburbs – the so-called dormitory suburbs – around Tokyo. As Kawamura often says an important concern in his theatre is "depicting the city." The city is revealing and expressive as a site of Japanese society and culture. What is important here is that the city that Kawamura depicts in *Hamletclone* is somewhat different from the city that he used to describe in the 1980s. As Uchino (2000) and Eckersall (2000) demonstrate, during the 1980s Kawamura was instrumental in the move to represent Tokyo as a site of millennial, science fiction-like anguish and postmodern dystopia (for example, inviting comparisons to *Blade Runner*, and the popular Japanese animation *Akira*). However, in *Hamletclone*, the city is closely related to the family and is represented as the site of nostalgia for a bygone era and fabled dreams of middle class people. We might say that *Hamletclone* is the story of the end of the dream of suburbia.

If this is so, how can we define the space of suburbia in *Hamletclone*? What is suburbia like in this drama? To answer this question we should return our attention to the character of the Old Gay Prince and ask who exactly is this character? Why is he sitting there, behind the audience throughout the play? From the position of the audience he can't be seen and our attention is focused on the action on the stage. But we never fail to hear his voice through a microphone. The source of this voice in *Hamletclone* seems full of uncertainty, to the extent that the voice may sound like the voice of a phantom. One can imagine this is just like a voice that Prince Hamlet in Shakespeare's play might have heard rising from under the ground – that is, the voice of the former king. In this sense the space of suburbia in *Hamletclone* is strangely skewed – with the attention of its inhabitants focused on one thing (such as consumption), while authority is distant and panoptic (seeing from behind) yet, at the same time, strangely weak and phantasmic.

In an interview preceding the first performance of *Hamletclone*, Kawamura said that the Gay Prince was a kind of Japanese Emperor figure and that the play was designed to be the Prince's imagined narrative and commentary on the state of Japan (Kawamura 2000b). Although there is no clear statement on Japan's "Emperor system" in this play, we should note that the Gay Prince (the man who says that he was once Hamlet) and the Thief signify a duality. They work in counterpoint to signify power in Japan. That is to say, the Gay Prince is eager to give up the role of Hamlet while the Thief is eager to attain it. The Thief refers to life in the commuter towns and his own dysfunctional family housed somewhere in the Tokyo suburbs. His familiarity with this life suggests that he belongs to the Japanese middle-class

suburban sprawl. In aspiring to the name of Hamlet, the Thief symbol-
ically serves as an object of the collective desire for the stable, comfortable existence that is a commonplace idea of the nuclear family
among Japan's middle-classes. They seek solace in their continued quiet
and orderly lives while at the same time they have become more of
endangered species as a result of increased social problems; for
example, anti-social and psychopathic behaviour, increased levels of un-
employment and reduced living standards following the end to
economic prosperity in 1989. In other words, the middle class themselves are made phantasmic and seemly unreal.

In regard to the idea of the middle-class (the bourgeoisie), Marx
writes:

> [T]hey can't represent themselves, they must be represented. Their repre-
> sentative must at the same time appear as their master, as an authority over
> them, as an unlimited governmental power that protects them against the
> other classes and sends them rain and sunshine from above. (Marx 1979:
> 187-8)

What is interesting from this statement is that, in *Hamletclone*,
Kawamura seems to use the idea of Bonapartism that Marx once used in
his analysis of the Second Empire in France. In this sense, the Thief in
the play is a symbolic figure of male workers (salary men, an alienated
bourgeoisie) who live in modern suburbs all over the country. For them,
Prince Hamlet appears as an authority that compensates for their sense
of oppression and lost dreams. Marx describes Louis Bonaparte
(Napoleon III) as a phantom that roams here and there in the decentred
space of nascent democracy. Although Kawamura has made no direct
reference to Marx, his drawing of Hamlet seems to be a counterpart to
the supreme power of the Second Empire. For instance, in *Hamletclone*,
the relationship among the Gay Prince, Horatio, and the young neo-
fascist seems to mirror the relationship between Louis Bonaparte and his
well-known secret political society; the Society of the Tenth of
December. As Walter Benjamin remarks, a society "whose cadres,
according to Marx, had been supplied by 'the whole indeterminate,
disintegrated, fluctuating mass which the French call *la boheme*'"
(Benjamin 1973: 12).

While such an image is of absolute power we should also take into
account the fact that Hamlet in *Hamletclone* is a person who constantly
wants to give up playing his role (hence "I was Hamlet"... etc). In other
words, Kawamura depicts the space of suburbia here as a complete
dispersal of power wherein not even a despot can rule in any meaningful
sense. Thus, at the beginning of this drama, the Prince composite
character played by the three actors (male, female, cross-dressed) says,

"I was Adolf Hitler. / I was Josef Stalin. / I was Pol Pot...." The possibility of revolution or social change, as well as the possibility for some kind of new despotism, remains forever suspended in this play. Thus, Kawamura said:

> I think that in this drama I am always telling a kind of the story of an imagined civil war in Tokyo. But, at the same time, I really feel like such an event is absolutely impossible in this city now." (Kawamura 2000b)

In *Hamletclone*, the system of political representation malfunctions everywhere. At the end of this drama, a political party, which consists of "bogus high schoolgirls," carries out a revolution and quickly succeeds in establishing a new government. They are seemingly able to "represent themselves" as political subjects in this scene. However, what matters here is that this revolutionary action thoroughly lacks a sense of reality. In the later part of *Hamletclone*, an image is triumphantly projected onto the screen to indicate the success of their *coup d'état*. It is a fake picture of the new cabinet, where the schoolgirls with their faces painted black and their lips white – a well-known fashion among Tokyo schoolgirls in the late 1990s – are drawn up in lines on the entrance steps of the Prime Minister's residence. Certainly Kawamura intends this as a joke, but he also insinuates that such a thing is impossible. In this play Kawamura repeatedly cites the lines from Müller's *Hamletmachine*: "I am not Hamlet. ... My drama doesn't happen anymore."

There is no doubt then, that the space of suburbia in *Hamletclone* is marked by a frustration with the possibility of being political. Instead the play explores the sense of apathy and powerlessness that is shared by Japanese people. After a series of sterile political battles, the Gay Prince says in his last monologue:

> But happiness only comes to the land that has forgotten the word (happiness). As long as we mention the word (happiness) the civil war of the suburbs continues. (Kawamura 2000a)

In other words, the potential of being political is always reduced to the desperate drive of the collapsing family.

Here also Kawamura succeeds in responding to Müller's *Hamletmachine*. In *Hamletmachine*, Müller writes a striking image of a political riot in East Germany (or somewhere similar), wherein the narrator "I" experiences a sense of duality in the political space. He feels empathy for both the demonstrators and the soldiers simultaneously. Thus Müller's well-known critique of subjectivity and revolutionary politics reads:

> ... the government brings in troops, tanks. My place, if my drama would still happen, would be both sides of the front, between the frontlines, over

and above them. I stand in the stench of the crowd and hurl stones at police-men, soldiers, tanks, bullet-proof glass. I look through the double doors of bullet-proof glass at the crowd pressing forward and smell the sweat of my fear. Choking with nausea, I shake my fist at myself who stands behind the bullet-proof glass. Shaking with fear and contempt, I see myself in a crowd pressing forward, foaming at the mouth, shaking my fist at myself. (Müller 1984: 56)

It is certain that even as Kawamura is inspired by such an image, he is also aware that this sense of political turmoil is unlikely to happen in present-day Tokyo. In this respect, *Hamletclone* might suggest the same viewpoint as Hirata Oriza, popular "quiet theatre movement"(*shizuka na engeki*) of the 1990s, that steadfastly depicts the apolitical postures of Japanese people in their everyday life. Furthermore, when asked about his attitude to Müller's text in view of his own politics, Kawamura states: "I think that to emphasise the aspect of anti-establishmentism in *Hamletclone* is not necessarily suitable for the current Japanese histor-ical context." (Kawamura 2000b) Instead, as has been mentioned above, Kawamura emphasises the significance of depicting a singular man of power, such as the Emperor even if his depiction takes the form of a composite characterisation in his play. Thus, Kawamura continues:

As for the Emperor system, I also feel that what is the most important task for Japanese playwrights today is not to write about the Emperor system, but to write a play in which the Emperor appears as a character. A play without the Emperor seems still insufficient to me. (Kawamura 2000b)

Why is the appearance of the Emperor indispensable? Without the Gay Prince-Emperor figure, for instance, *Hamletclone* would have been no more than a melodramatic description of negative aspects of sub-urban families; depictions that are too often seen on television or in theatres. In order to comment critically on and intervene in present social conditions in Japan, Kawamura introduces a phantom-like repre-sentation of a dictator, one similar to Louis Bonaparte, Hitler, Hirohito and so on. This is related to his notion of the cultural space of suburbia. For Kawamura, suburbia is a space where phantoms of domination and oppression roam about. In this case the city of Tokyo, which also featured centrally in an earlier Kawamura work called *Tokyo Trauma* (1995), can be read as a suburban authoritarian dystopia as well. In *Tokyo Trauma* all the characters nightmarishly behave as if they were possessed by a phantom ideology based on the collective memory of Japanese militarism. If we were to compared this space to Beckett's existential void, for example, then Kawamura's view of suburbia is of a space where "people are unconsciously waiting for an autocrat, but he never comes." The Thief is a man who ceases to be a father, and that's all. He will never be an autocrat, though he will never stop desiring to be one. On the other hand, the Gay Prince is a Father who ceases to be a man; he always changes his sex in order to evade being a figure of patriarchy, though he never ceases to be a phantom of the patriarchal order. One might reflect on the position of the Japanese Emperor in this regard, who has become a figure of lesser authoritarianism, more suburban and "one with the people," at least in image if not substance.

Hamletclone concludes with a scene of the Thief alone on stage into which the voice of the Gay Prince intrudes:

> A civil war breaks out on the streets. The Thief shoots the Gay Prince sitting in the tower.
>
> **Old Gay Prince:** Then I collapse. I am shot by a nameless assassin. The bullet penetrates my left lung and a new emptiness is born. My auto-biography is now complete. The title is the "The birth of a nation." (Kawamura 2000a)

The monologue suggests that the Thief will never kill the phantom, and the phantom of Hamlet will never disappear. That is to say, the Thief will never be perfectly represented nor embodied by some authority and will inevitably have to play with the phantom limbs of authority forever.

Such a vision is deeply pessimistic, but remarkably, also reflects the present Japanese political situation. There is little doubt that many Japanese people – who typically don't support any particular political party – are caught in a tension that oscillates between possibility and impossibility in regard to effective political representation. There is a feeling that they are unable to participate in political debates and gain some sense of representing themselves. This is especially the case for urban Japan. In this regard, *Hamletclone* points to a kind of patriarchal closure that is closely related to the malfunction of political represen-tation. As with the opening moments of *Hamletclone*, this sense of closure is often represented metaphorically by the theatricalised image of the "concentration camp" in Kawamura's work. In wanting to be represented by some kind of authority, people seem ineluctably drawn into an authoritarian rule. Kawamura wants to suggest in this image that Japanese society is (once again) confronted with the danger of becoming trapped in, or entranced by, a kind of dictatorship. This, in turn, is nothing but the continuance of patriarchy. Even if the Japanese middle classes attempt to intervene in political processes and gain a sense of representation, it is difficult to avoid escaping the domination of the phantom of the patriarch.

There is, however, another outcome that *Hamletclone* suggests, one that might allow for a sense of escape from the phantoms of despotic and patriarchal rule. To conclude, we should consider the presence of women in Kawamura's play. What about the radical strategy of "becoming woman"? Just as Müller places Ophelia side by side with Hamlet, Kawamura finds in the figure of Ophelia the possibility for some acute and pivotal social change. Thus, he privileges her existence and extends the feminist mode through a notion of becoming woman as is symbolised in the figure of the transvestite Prince. In *Hamletclone*, Ophelia becomes a symbol of resistance, a party leader and a figurehead for the bogus high-school girls. But how does this approach unfold in Kawamura's play?

As mentioned above, under Ophelia's command these girls form a revolutionary government. I noted the obvious lack of a sense of reality to this manoeuvre, to the extent that they seem to be another phantasm in the play. Even so, we should note that this is a phantom of resistance – a phantom as a cultural Other to the patriarchal system.

However, Kawamura's use of Ophelia as an image of resistance is not without problems. Eckersall, for example, has contested Kawamura's sense of feminist politics and points to the weakness of female characters of his play *The Lost Babylon* (1999). Thus he writes:

> Who or what the women screenwriter [one of the main characters of this drama] represents is not resolved. Kawamura suggests that the character is a critique of representations of women in Japanese popular culture, "where women gaining power" is depicted as a woman toting a piece. Kawamura cites *Thelma and Louise* as a work widely viewed in Japan as a commentary on women's self-empowerment. But, as he argues, "even if women have guns that does not mean that they have power." The screenwriter in *Babylon* remains disempowered, gun and all. She belongs to the romantic fiction that she writes; her behaviour is conventionally feminine. She is presented rather than critically investigated." (Eckersall 2000: 106)

I think that the same is true in *Hamletclone*. The costume that these "revolutionaries" wear is a commonplace school uniform for girls, but a dress code that is often used to provoke sexual desires among men. This is especially the case in Japanese subcultural representations of the feminine, a milieu that Kawamura also sees himself working within. In support of Kawamura's stance, we might read this drama as a counter-attack by women, who by highlighting the strictures of a sexualised gaze can accuse men of their implicitly patriarchal social control. However, if the patriarchal system is solid and ruthlessly oppressive then victory against it is not easy to gain. That victory will inevitably be some romantic fiction that people can enjoy and consume only in their fantasy. To this end, the sudden victory in *Hamletclone* by the White Stalk revolutionaries only manages to suggest Kawamura's wish to break down the existing social system. It does not go so far as to investigate the real situation of women. Kawamura argues that the strange make-up favoured by schoolgirls in Tokyo at present (which is ghoulish and gothic) is interesting because it does not seem to intend to attract male desire. (Kawamura 2000b) However, as Eckersall says, "Kawamura's characters reveal considerable confusion about feminism." (2000: 106) In conclusion I think that feminism is not limited to a mere desire to reject the existing system.

Notwithstanding this point, there is no doubt that *Hamletclone* is an important work, one that clearly describes Japan's present situation of political crisis. It is also one that affects a hybrid; through the effective use of the ideas of Heiner Müller, Kawamura makes a powerful statement about the contradictions embedded into (indeed impossibility of) the Japanese political system in the present day.

Works Cited

Benjamin, Walter. *Charles Baudelaire: A Lyric Poet in the Era of High Capitalism.* London: Verso, 1973.

Eckersall, Peter. "Japan and Dystopia: Kawamura Takeshi's Daisan Erotica," *The Drama Review* 44. 1. (2000): 97-108.

Kawamura, Takeshi. *Hamletclone*. Tokyo: Ronsôsha, 2000a.

Kawamura, Takeshi. "Interview with author," n. p., 2000b.

Marx, Karl. "The Eighteenth Brumaire of Louis Bonaparte," *Collected Works* (vol. 11), by K. Marx and F. Engels. London: Lawrence and Wishart, 1979.

Müller, Heiner. *Hamletmachine and Other Texts for the Stage.* New York: Performing Arts Journal Publications, 1984.

Senda, Akihiko. *Gendai Engeki no Kôkai.* Tokyo: Riburopôrto, 1988.

Uchino, Tadashi. "Images of Armageddon: Japan's 1980s Theatre Culture," *The Drama Review* 44. 1. (2000): 85-96.

CHAPTER 7

Rhizomatic Dramaturgy:
Alternative Performance Practices

Denise VARNEY

This chapter suggests some possibilities for the theorisation of alternative theatre practice through Deleuzian concepts that help with both the articulation and critique of experimental performance. Within the context of the *Journey to Con-Fusion* project, alternative theatre practice refers to performance that is created through collaborative processes, that experiments with aesthetic, technical and cultural difference, and that deconstructs logocentric notions of representation and the subject. The co-existence of these alternatives and their sites of intersection suggests a further element: the rehearsal and the performance space as a plane of consistency for the interplay of difference.

Before proceeding with the discussion, I will first set out some selected moments from the performances I saw in both Melbourne and Tokyo. Memories of the live performance have been refreshed through viewing unedited videotapes, made but not published by the companies for the purposes of documentation only.

Part One

Members of both companies perform David Pledger's gestural choreography, a sequence of movements for the body suggestive of a code. The same sequence is repeated several times so that the spectator begins to discern differences of nuance, shape, size, emphasis, speed and intensity. A sequence of the same is dispersed among a multiplicity of bodies in space. (*Journey to Con-Fusion 1*, Open Stage, University of Melbourne, 1999. See Photo Essay by Miyauchi Katsu, Chapter 10)

Part Two

Performers move through space. Each performer is different but connected through a shared rhythm, a fixed gaze and an intense absorption. These are points of consistency. The differences are between a robotic, puppet-like performer that appears along side another that is searching and wondrous, light-footed and luminous in the light; another moves with skin taut and stretched like rubber. An older, heavier catatonicised body is filled with intensity and has retreated deep within its layers of skin, muscle and organ.

The sequence finishes. Another starts up in a different part of the space. Performers disappear into the dark corners and the light illuminates three other figures who react to their own media images on a screen. They are European actors and on the screen they recall emotional memories. The banality of personal memory is revealed in the drawn-out length of the sequence and its disconnection from narrative.

A European body lies on a bier-like structure. There is a solemn funeral procession. A flailing body begins thrashing to the sound of moaning, followed by a dirge and then grief. Bodies in overcoats on their haunches rock back and forwards.

A woman in an overcoat with a rucksack wanders through the space.

Loud techno music ruptures the space and performers jerk their bodies in rhythmic violence. And still the woman in the rucksack. A young woman laughs and cracks the space.

The question is how to theorise the performance without pinning it down, without stabilising it and fixing it to a place in aesthetics, in history and in culture.

(*Journey to Con-Fusion 2*, Morishita Studios, Tokyo 2000. See Photo Essay by Miyauchi Katsu, Chapter 10)

Part Three

A woman, traumatised, shudders slowly across the space. She is technique and affect. Two men dance the tango – one in white shirt and trousers, the other larger man in a white singlet and trousers.

This third phase of the project is a more confidant and developed showing of difference and fusion.

Pairs of performers embrace and then one throws the other violently against a wall. The action is repeated and the sound of the body on the wall fills the studio space.

(*Journey to Con-Fusion 3*, Dancehouse, Melbourne 2002. See Figs. One and Two, following this essay)

                                        ***

At the Morishita Studios in Tokyo, NYID artistic director David Pledger describes the collaboration between the two companies as a "meeting" and a "gathering of information." These words are carefully chosen and suggestive of an attitude of enquiry, of investigation and of exchange between two different parties. This is accentuated by the notion of a "meeting" implying that likeness as well as difference will form some kind of assemblage, in the Deleuzian sense, of a form without a central point or organising unity. "Gathering" suggests the gatherer, the collector and the nomad of a pre-consumerist society who searches and finds rather than purchases ready-made objects. Pledger continues to describe the project as a finding out about each other in terms of professional, social and cultural differences. There has been the attempt to *understand* something (is this to create knowledge?) about each other's theatres and processes of making theatre. Pledger also describes the collaboration as a crossing-over of sensibility and practice. Hence the immanent and desired con-fusion that arises.

Gekidan Kaitaisha artistic director, Shinjin Shimizu does not admit to difference, only to bodies and to the problem of space. His vision is of immanence: there is no outside of the performance, no transcendental point from which the subject sees and knows the object of the gaze. Shimizu, like Pledger, notices the common language of gesture, of bodies and of movement – suggestive of bodies in a process of change. There is no transcendent reality for Shimizu, unless it is the "the inhumanness of the 'diabolical powers'" from which there is no escape (Deleuze & Guattari 1986: 12).

If there is a text or root-book that each company brings to the collaboration then it is concealed, even discarded in favour of memorised sequences of movement and action. The politics of the directors, however, will be surveyed and mapped by and onto the performers. They undergo confusion, not only in the challenge of language, but also in the challenge of processing two directors and their distinctive working methods, both of which must be fathomed in a short period of time. This will constrain any propensity towards either director playing the General marking out and defending his territory. The performers rewrite the directors' instructions in the workshops, many of which are open to the public, and in the performances, which take place with the audience seated among or at least close to the performers. The problem of artistic form that lies between two companies, two directors, and other binaries such as two cultures and performance traditions will be partially resolved through the affirmative accommodation and translation of difference.

The affirmation of difference, as well as its accommodation and translation, brings me to the language of Deleuze and Guattari. Their concepts, words, metaphors and/or terms – the rhizome, becoming, assemblage and nomadology – elaborated in *A Thousand Plateaux*, offer the theorist a language that follows the spirit of alternative performance without pinning it down to a grid made up of category, genre and form. The impetus for applying these terms to aesthetic practice comes from Deleuze and Guattari's reading of Kafka's novels and their references to the nineteenth century dramatist Georg Büchner, whose writing they describe as rhizomatic (Deleuze and Guattari 1986 & 1994: 25).

The Deleuzian rhizome refers to the botanical subterranean stem or tuber that spreads in all directions like couch grass and weeds. It is also a burrow with several points of entrance and exit and a capacity to function in multiple ways such as "shelter, supply, movement, evasion and breakout" (Deleuze and Guattari 1996: 7). These natural objects are used as metaphors for an alternative mode of thought and action that offers an escape from traditional hierarchical, linear, fixed structures figured as the tree of knowledge for example. The rhizome offers a way of further articulating the alternative dimension of the *Journey to Con-Fusion* Project. Public performances are described by Pledger in Tokyo as "performances/public showings," that is to say, they are a showing of work that is ongoing and incomplete; always ready to be picked up again. Beginning in Melbourne in December 1999, continuing in Tokyo in July 2000 and picked up again in May 2002, the work could conceivably go on and on. Within the performance, action starts up at various seemingly random locations on the floor. There are very few entrances and exits for the performers. They can sit on a chair and suddenly dissolve into fluidity, falling and dissolving into space. A light or a sound starts up and a new offshoot begins to make its way through the space opening up a different performance trajectory. In *Journey to Con-Fusion 3*, there are multiple walls within the walls of the studio, framed by light and shade, against which victims are thrown. There is no architectural logic to the placement of the walls and they soon disappear only for the action to start up somewhere else. The performers are always ready to enter another sequence. This dramaturgy suggest the rhizomatic mode: "A rhizome may be broken, shattered at a given spot, but it will start up again on one of its lines, or on new lines (Deleuze and Guattari 1994: 9).

But how is the dramaturgy rhizomatic and therefore different from the old techniques of improvised performance and impulse work on the one hand and the *Butô* tradition of the other? There are similarities and differences. The similarities lie in the apparent randomness of the actions and the discipline of bodies immersed in technique. But the crucial differences lie in the fragmentation of the impulse and the disciplined body. The performers do not see an impulse through from beginning to completion. Rather, it is interrupted. Thrash music, ordered by Shimizu, ruptures the interiority of the disciplined performer at one with a rhythm. There is no giving oneself over to the impulse or technique but rather a taut wariness of what external factor will hit next. The intrusiveness of light, sound, a mediatised image or violent confrontation fragments the inner unity of impulse and improvisation and the rigid adherence to a master discipline.

The components of the anti-hierarchical, non-linear, disconnected rhizome, of "lines of articulation or segmentarity, strata and territories" are tantalisingly present (Deleuze and Guattari 1994: 3). In the journey without beginning or end that is the performance of *The Journey to Con-Fusion*, the performances are not the privileged end-products, as in the creation or production of the performance as object. Rather, the public performance is another segment of the project, immanent within the playing out of the project in all its differences.

In its affirmative mode, the rhizome is a series of connections, lines of flight, movements, comparative rates of flow, acceleration and rupture. In the description of a sequence from *Journey to Con-Fusion 2*, a slow and solemn funeral procession is ruptured by a flailing, thrashing body and accompanied by a mass of hunched wailing bodies. This outburst accelerates as the bier is carried away and the moaning gives way to a thrash metal sequence of bodies rhythmically thrashing to the sound. Together, the departing funeral procession, if that is what it is, and the thrash metal sequence, resist narrativisation or semiosis as well as classical unity and balance. The asymmetrical dimensions form an "*assemblage* " of multiplicity, intensities and supplements (Deleuze and Guattari 1994: 4). In the rhizomatic mode, these elements replace representation, text, signification and reference, yet there is also the possibility of the act of meaning-making, if that is desired.

The performances are in themselves a form of escape from contemporary Australia and Japan and their respective and collective histories and in this sense they evoke the Deleuzian becoming. By the second stage of the project, there is the sense of a temporary escape from Australia by the academics who journey to Tokyo (Eckersall *et al.* 2001: 71-86). By stage three in 2002, refugees seeking asylum have been detained in detention centres in Australia. The throwing of the victim against the wall sequence described above is both a reference to the violence in the detention centres and a mode of escape through performance from its empirical truth. The performers engage in an act of becoming-guard and becoming-refugee. The audience undergoes a becoming-silent witness. Each becoming is both a reference to and an escape from cognitive truth through the symbolic. In their reading of Kafka's novella, *The Metamorphosis*, Deleuze and Guattari describe Gregor's metamorphosis into a dung beetle as a becoming-animal. It is a line of escape, "an intense line of flight" to a place where the subject is no longer interpellated by his father/employer/state (Deleuze and Guattari 1986: 14).

What if the performance is considered a series of becomings? It would no longer be representational but reactive, transformative and subversive. This would seem to offer an answer to the question of how we understand and critically respond to a performance that resists taking an ideological or aesthetic position and that indeed ruptures the relation between sign and referent. What drives a performance that is investigative and experimental? How to take hold of open-ended possibilities?

It is in the light of these questions that the deployment of Deleuzian concepts helps politicise the open-ended performance. The affinity between the performances and the language of Deleuze and Guattari offers some assurance, at the very least, of the creative and subversive possibilities of the project. Hitching the *Journey to Con-Fusion* project to the Deleuzian project and finding a fit between them, if not a rhizomatic connection, helps identify the alternative aspect of the work and its resistance to dominant modes of representation that are oppressive in their imposition of meaning and form.

To return to the second sequence cited above. A European body lies on a bier while a Japanese body flails. Moreover, the European body is female and the Japanese body is male. She is serene in her stillness, her body composed, emptied. His body appears as a body without organs flapping in a loose overcoat; his individuality is undifferentiated. The overdetermined signs are suggestive but open-ended. Is this a performance of the death of the European subject, or is the performance blind to ethnicity and gender? Is this the construction of an intercultural moment? Is there a contrast in modes of grief? In another sequence, as already mentioned, three European performers, a woman and two men, perform the technique of emotion memory. A video projects their vocalisation of childhood memories as their bodies in the present of the performance, through lying still, relive the affect. This performance of emotional memory, a formation of the Stanislavski system as it is popularly practised in the West, is disconnected from the realism it is supposed to create. It is stripped of any given circumstances, of building a character and of creating a role. In the meantime, the Japanese performers follow lines of intensity and distension derived from *Butô* training techniques. The catatonicised unseeing cross-eyed *Butô* body intersects with the emoting tearful face of Western realism. There are dimensions rather than layers of meaning. The compositions appear as sites of intersection and asymmetry through which meaning pushes but is not ingrained.

The *Journey to Con-Fusion* project shows bodies under pressure, flashing through a range of partially and never-fully formed subjectivities: bent double dragging a suitcase; in a coat with a rucksack; cross-dressed in a dress; in corsets; in a g-string and high heels posing for a camera. In the latter example, the woman is young and slim with spiked hair and a face made up like a drag queen. She can almost look like a boy. She has a knife that she wields and as she poses she is a calendar girl, a body-builder, an Olympian, an eroticised body and a reclining nude, lit so that her skin is richly luminous. The performer divests herself of subjectivity and gives herself over to mobility and fluidity, ready to set off on any number of trajectories, both within the body and through the space. It is a body undergoing a number of becomings, including the post-human. For the performer in this mode of performance, the enacted subjectivity is a mode of becoming. That is, it is not a relation between actor and character, "becoming is neither one nor two, nor the relation of the two." The performance occurs in the grey matter between, "it is the in-between, the border or line of flight or descent running perpendicular to both" (Deleuze and Guattari 1994: 293).

Within the model of performance that I am theorising, the rhizomatic flows that occur in the performance are a way of "becoming" that brings the performance into view. Becoming in this sense is conducted amongst other subjects: collaborators, performers, technicians, spectators and critics, and the technologies of performance: space, light, sound and the reproduced image. This imaginative, creative post-human becoming gives the performance its intensity and power. Becoming as it is used in this context is a departure from the *loci* that legitimise the performer in his or her everyday life: the juridical, medicalised, surveyed, territorialised and nationalised citizen. The performer can be seen moving through multiple subjectivities thereby resisting classification, title, a fixed address and passport control.

But becomings are also corporeal and kinesic and involve visibility, action and sound. They happen through changes in gesture, movement, language, sound and speed. Becoming works on the particle or fragment rather than the actor's whole self. It does not demand the presence of the politicised performer, nor an integrated, whole or centred subject. Becoming allows for fragmented, split and multiple subjectivities to "enter into composition" with an image and then to disperse and move on. It provides a model of performance that sits well with the movement of the performance across time and space, where there is no such thing as a fixed point.

On this view, the performer enters into a becoming when he or she slips out of his or her self, or major identity, into performance. The performer undergoes a deterritorialisation of the self and becomes the construct of his or her action. In a radical rethinking of the relation between the performer and performance, the notion of becoming suggests that the categories of subject and object dissolve in the performance process. Becoming "is never imitating." Rather it is concerned with rhizomatic connections between subjectivities, objects and spaces.

Within the model I am describing the performers also appear to move between points, like nomads. Deleuze and Guattari's description of Nomadology draws on the mythical and imaginary nomad of pre-agrarian culture and in their usage is a non-individuated, decentred *haecceity*.[1] Thus the nomadic figuration is mobile, fluid and changeable. To follow the metaphor further, just as the nomads of the steppe do not travel between fixed points, there are variables that interrupt fixed destinations, the Deleuzian nomad does not follow a predetermined pathway between a starting point and a destination, or an origin and a goal. Rather, the nomad moves along pathways and trajectories. And most importantly, the nomad roams outside state and representational systems. In a description which is more metaphoric than anthropological, Deleuze and Guattari's nomad is a molecule that roams outside state systems (Deleuze and Guattari. 1994: 380). Beyond and outside state representational systems, nomads assemble rather than imitate.

These features suggest a connection between the notion of the nomad and the performer who steps outside the representational frame of text-based or naturalist and realist theatre, and personal and national identity. The nomadic performer, like the nomad, does not engage in an act of mimesis. He/she does not imitate a pre-existing textualised dramatic character's speech and gestures, but enacts or shows subjectivity in a state of flux. This is, perhaps, the space that is most appropriate to performance since modernism. Brian Massumi describes nomadic subjects as "immersed in a changing state of things." The nomad is not a subject who views the world as the object of its gaze; nomads "do not reflect upon the world" rather, they are in a constant process of generating worlds (Massumi 1994, xiii).

In terms of the *Journey to Con-Fusion* Project the performers, by virtue of their differences from each other and within their own layers of subjectivity, set off on different trajectories that call for a theorisation beyond those that we most often use. There are things that occur in performance, the smallest of movements, the catching of the breath, the intensity of a moment, that have to do with the transmission and

---

[1]   Deleuze and Guattari use this term as an alternative to identity, a coming together of different streams.

distribution of flows, desire, energies, activated through technique, and at its various points of reception, going past it.

The key to observing lines of nomadic processes in alternative performance is Braidotti's interpretation of the concept as an imaginary or fictive metaphor that describes an aesthetic style (Braidotti 1994). Thus in the *Journey to Con-Fusion* Project the nomadic style – consisting of rhizomatic flows and becomings – posits that movement and image flow from one to the other, effacing categories to make unlikely creative connections. These flows are performative in that they are becomings in time and space and indivisible into subject (performer) and object (performance). The "as if" (to use Braidotti's term) of performance allows for a certain mode of impersonation and even parody, where the theatrical performer plays with posed subjectivities as is readable in the image of the European body on the bier. There is in practice a distinguishing mode of impersonation and parody in NYID that differs from that of Gekidan Kaitaisha. The GK style has less self-reflexivity and a stronger sense of the body as moved by external powers generated by state institutions. It is "as if" for GK that external powers inhabit the body leaving little space for the distance parody requires. It is "as if" the repetition, the interruption and the abrupt changes in direction of the *Journey to Con-Fusion* project identify the differences within that transforms the performance from a one-way movement into several nomadic explorations.

The critic and the theorist might find that to read the performer as a nomad, who goes back and forth, and embodies repetition and reversal is useful for the discussion of the particular kinds of collaborations found in alternative theatre practice. The discourse of these per-formances would suggest that there is much to say for the putting of difference into theatrical space and letting it wander. This collaboration offers a mode of resistance to the totality of the same, of the imposed unities of aesthetics, style and form and to the indeterminacy of the hybrid.

Works Cited

Braidotti, R. *Nomadic Subjects*. New York: Columbia University Press, 1994.

Deleuze, G. and Guattari, F., *A Thousand Plateaus: Capitalism and Schizophrenia*. Trans. Brian Massumi. Minneapolis: University of Minnesota Press, 1994.

Deleuze, G. and Guattari, F., *Kafka: Toward a Minor Literature*. Trans. Dana Polan. Minneapolis & London: University of Minnesota Press, 1986.

Eckersall, P., Fensham, R., Scheer, E. and Varney, D. "Tokyo Diary," *Performance Research* 6 (2001): 71-86.

Fig. One: Greg Ufan, Kumamoto Kenjiro, *Journey to Con-Fusion 3* (2002)
Photo: Lyn Pool

Fig. Two: Kumamoto
Kenjiro, *Journey to Con-Fusion 3* (2002)
Photo: Lyn Pool

CHAPTER 8

Exhibiting the Past: The Japanese National War Museum and the Construction of Collective Memory

TAKAHASHI Yuichiro

Introduction

This essay attempts to analyse from a *performance studies* perspective the ways in which a museum display, as a *cultural performance*, is organized to serve the purpose of the maintenance of a dominant social discourse. The focus of the essay will be on a national history museum called Showa Hall, named after the late Emperor Showa (1900-1989), opened in 1999 in Tokyo. Although expectations were high that it would become the first national war museum in Japan to address squarely the issues of crimes against humanity committed by the Japanese military between 1931 and 1945, the decision taken by the government was to avoid all politically contentious issues. The museum was inaugurated with a publicly stated mission to teach for posterity how the Japanese had suffered during and after the war.

At the beginning of the essay, I will briefly demonstrate in what ways museums can be analysed as performance and cite a number of key concepts suggesting the ontology of a museum in the age of multiculturalism and postcolonialism. Then, before going into the discussion of Showa Hall, I will consider the difficulties of displaying war, using as an example the aborted *Enola Gay* exhibition planned for 1995 at the U.S. National Air and Space Museum in Washington D.C. The main objective of this essay is to offer a critique of the ways in which Showa Hall uses its mode of display to transform individual wartime memories into a single and coherent narrative and thus to construct a homogeneous *collective memory* of a nation.

Museum Display as Performance

The theatrical nature of museum display is aptly put by Barbara Kirshenblatt-Gimblett when she says, "[e]xhibitions are fundamentally theatrical, for they are how museums perform the knowledge they create (Kirshenblatt-Gimblett 1998: 3)." The significance of her remark lies in the notions that museums create (rather than explicate) the knowledge that they display, and do so by performative means. Institutional authority of large public and private museums allows them to perform by selecting the objects of display, defining them, detaching them from their original contexts, re-contextualising them in a museum space, framing and defamiliarising them for the spectatorial gaze of observers. Collections, before they are publicly displayed, are subjected to a process of numerous selections, of being spatially arranged and adorned, placed in different types of showcases, under different types of lighting, and with explanatory panels of varying size and conspicuousness attached. The analogous process is observable in the theatre where play-texts are selected, casts auditioned, sets designed, and only after a lengthy rehearsal period, the audience is allowed to watch a show. Museum curators, like theatre directors, work on the consciousness of the viewer by manipulating the objects of display.

Kirshenblatt-Gimblett's term "performance epistemology" (Kirshenblatt-Gimblett 1998: 194), which she uses in relation to the function of museums, shapes the bodily experience of visitors as visceral, kinaesthetic, haptic, and intimate. This echoes Foucauldian notions of power and knowledge, which subjugates, through intricate and complex exercises of power in net-like organizations, human agencies into docile bodies (Foucault 1977, 1980). Althusser considers a museum as a form of state ideological apparatuses that *interpellate* visitors to assign them an identity of a subject (Althusser 1971). Regarding the subject itself, Judith Butler's notion that both gender and sexual identities are constructed through an iteration of performative acts has made a tremendous impact on performance studies (Butler 1990a, 1990b). Richard Schechner, who takes a "broad spectrum approach" to performance studies (Schechner 1990: 15), considers that "[e]verything from gender to city planning to the presentations of self in everyday life is 'constructed' [as] a 'play of surfaces and effects,' which is to say: performed" (Schechner 2000).

Recent museum practitioners, who are becoming increasingly conscious of the performative nature of museum display, have, for some time, been questioning the traditionally sanctioned role of museums as an arbiter of knowledge. As today's post-colonial condition demands from museums dialogical and polyphonic articulations, they are now less concerned with the canonical reconstruction of a *grand récit*. Already in the 1991 anthology entitled *Exhibiting Cultures: The Poetics and Politics of Museum Display*, the editors Ivan Karp and Steven D. Lavine announced their conviction that "now few serious museum practitioners would claim that a museum could be anything but a forum" (Karp and Lavine 1991: 3). In the companion volume *Museum and Communities: The Politics of Public Culture*, using a similar spatial metaphor, Karp reiterated the notion of the exhibition as a political arena in which "definitions of identity and culture are asserted and contested" (Karp 1992: 1). James Clifford, while being aware of the kind of pressure that communities are likely to assert on museums to "adapt to the taste of their assumed audience," nevertheless envisions future museums as "contact zone," as "specific places of transit, inter-cultural borders, contexts of struggle and communication between discrepant communities" (Clifford 1988: 213).[1]

From a performance studies point of view, Richard Schechner's concept of "environmental theatre" (Schechner 1973) offers a model for the museums to come. Schechner coined the term from the experiments he had with the Performance Group, an avant-garde theatre collective that he led in the late 1960s and the early 70s. Inside a traditional theatre building, where a proscenium arch separates the space of the stage from that of the audience, the members of the audience can neither participate in the stage action nor alter the firmly controlled reading of the play offered by the director. They remain passive "voyeurs" intent to watch what is going on behind the fourth wall. Instead of presenting his works in an enclosed "theatre" where the prevalent gaze is that of the audience looking unidirectionally at the stage, Schechner experimented with an open "environment" which may be created in an interior of a building but may also be found on streets or in nature. In an "environmental theatre," actions take place not only on the front "stage," but simultaneously everywhere, behind, within, or surrounding the audience. Freedom of movement given to the members of audience heightens the consciousness of their bodies. Creation of such a space makes multi-focused staging and polyphonic articulations possible. Conceptualising museums as "environmental theatre" frees visitors from the obligation of being interpellated by the objects of display and allows them to negotiate their own positionalities *vis-à-vis* historically and politically contingent display.

---

[1]   Clifford borrows the term "contact zone" from Mary Louise Pratt's study of nineteenth century women's travel writings (Pratt 1992).

The "Enola Gay" Exhibition at the U.S. National Air and Space Museum

It is, however, often the case that external pressures thwart the efforts of museum practitioners, especially when dealing with politically contentious issues. When the interests of a community that is represented by a museum are at risk, power often intervenes. As a result, minority groups that the majority regards as "other" are denied a space to articulate themselves, or at most allowed a token representation to feign a "politically correct" appearance. The display often becomes exclusionary when it touches on the issues of gender, sexual, ethnic, or historical identity of a certain group. The question I would like to pose before going into the discussion of Showa Hall, is whether it is still possible to represent minority voices when the subject of an exhibition is a collective memory of a nation, an "imagined community" according to Benedict Anderson's oft-quoted definition (Anderson 1983). As a case study, I would like to consider briefly the cancelled *Enola Gay* exhibition at the Smithsonian Institution's U.S. National Air and Space Museum, planned for the fiftieth anniversary of the victory over Japan, because the expectations and disappointments that accompanied the exhibition were shared by many at the inauguration of Showa Hall.

Enola Gay is a B-29 bomber that dropped an atom bomb on Hiroshima in August 1945. Air Force veterans had long been campaigning that the aircraft be restored to its original condition and put on public display. Partly responding to their call, the National Air and Space Museum planned an exhibition entitled "The Crossroads: The End of World War Two, the Atomic Bomb and the Origins of the Cold War," in which the fuselage of the bomber was to be the main exhibit. The museum's intention was to review the use of an atom bomb from an historical perspective, by asking the viewers to consider its implications and to reflect, not only on the glory achieved, but also on the horror unleashed by the bombing mission.

As soon as the proposal was announced, the same people who demanded the display of the bomber in the first place raised opposition. Opposition by the Air Force Association, a powerful lobbying organisation for the U.S. Air Force, was soon joined by the American Legion, members of Congress, and the national media, which portrayed the museum curators as anti-American academics campaigning for a politically correct version of history.[2] When repeated revisions and

---

[2]   U.S. Republican Senator Thad Cochran commented that a national museum "shouldn't be used by revisionist historians to try to change the facts of World War

rounds of negotiations failed to convince the Air Force Association, the exhibition was cancelled and the director of the museum, Martin Harwit, resigned. In the place of the themed and nuanced exhibition that had been planned, the restored *Enola Gay* was made available for public viewing, with no commentary attached at a museum annex at Dulles International Airport outside Washington D.C. Smithsonian Secretary Michael Heyman admitted the mistake they had made of trying to honour veterans while presenting a balanced view of history. In his words, "[the veterans] were not looking for analysis and, frankly, we did not give enough thought to the intense feelings such an analysis would evoke" (Stone 1995: 1). Historian Mike Wallace observes that museum goers do not want to see "the exhibits that dismantle the mythic dramas that give meaning and value to their lives" (Wallace 1997: 125). And Richard Kurin, director of the Smithsonian's Centre for Folklife Programs, believes that the exhibition failed because the museum neglected to respect those who would be represented in it. It offered veterans "a history that was not of their memory, and also a history that was not how they wanted to be remembered" (Kurin 1997: 80). This issue of who would be represented and how, was also central to the display at Showa Hall.

History Wars: Memories of Japanese Imperialism

Japan's first war museums post 1945 were built in 1955 in Hiroshima and Nagasaki, where a large population had been decimated by atom bomb attacks. In 1975, three years after its sovereignty was returned to Japan, another museum was opened on the island of Okinawa, where one of the fiercest ground battles in the Pacific left more than 100,000 civilians dead, compared to the military tolls of 85,000 Japanese and 15,000 Americans. Those museums had a clear purpose of appeasing the dead and making a plea for peace.

Most Japanese, however, for many years after the war, had uncertain attitudes about how they should come to terms with the memories of it. The majority opted for selective amnesia, remembering their own

---

Two" (Stone 1995: 1). The Wall Street Journal claimed in its editorial that "the American museum whose business is to tell the nation's story is now in the hands of academics unable to view American history as anything other than a woeful catalogue of crimes and aggressions against the helpless peoples of the earth" (Kohn 1996: 161).

suffering but consigning to oblivion atrocities committed either by themselves or by other Japanese.[3]

In the early 1990s, however, records documenting atrocities committed by the Japanese began to be unearthed. NGOs both in and outside Japan made active campaigns demanding compensation and an apology from the Japanese government. In particular, the testimonies made by former "comfort women" who were forced into sexual slavery by the Japanese military fuelled the public anger.[4] Memories of the war became a focus of intense debates.

On the other hand, the conservative government and its right wing supporters have tried to revive nationalist sentiments. In their view, aggression has been justified as necessary military action to defend Japan's interests. Some even wish to portray Japan as a liberator of Asia from Western colonialism. In 1982, the Ministry of Education censors ordered publishers of school textbooks to use the word "advancement" to describe the invasion of China, and "riot" for the pro-independence rally organised in Korea. Although strong protests by China and Korea forced the ministry to retract the order, the incident gave a momentum to the Chinese and the Koreans to display history from their own perspectives. In 1985, two new museums, the Nanjing Massacre Memorial and the Korean Independence Hall were inaugurated.

In the late 1990s, the revisionist tendency was accelerated by a group of scholars who criticised the teaching of what they called a self-incriminating or a masochistic view of history. They claimed that history taught in schools was prejudiced and was depriving children of opportunities to manifest healthy and spontaneous nationalism.

With these developments as background, the early 1990s saw the construction of a number of war museums in Japan, mostly by municipal or prefectural governments. Although some avoided an explicitly accusatory tone of language, they have generally portrayed Japan as an

---

[3]   Regarding the question of guilt, a double standard exists in Japanese foreign and domestic policies. By accepting the verdict of the Tokyo War Tribunals, Japan assumed full responsibility for the war. But the end of the war also meant Japan's swift incorporation into the Cold War structure as a Western ally. Immunity was granted to the Emperor. And when the execution of a few army chiefs was over, remaining charges of war crimes were dropped. Admission of guilt became domestically an obsolete subject.

[4]   Until the 1992 discovery of documents that proved otherwise, the government had stubbornly denied their involvement in military brothels, saying that they were operated by private entrepreneurs (as commercial prostitution was legal in Japan at the time).

aggressor nation during the Asia-Pacific War between 1931 and 1945. The museums in Osaka and Kyoto have made it their special commitment to display Japanese atrocities. These museums invite visitors to approach history both from the victim's and the victimiser's points of view and engage in reflexive re-examination of the country's past.

Planning Showa Hall: Japan's First National War Museum

But the story behind the construction of Showa Hall was different. Showa Hall is state-owned but independently run by a private foundation, the Japan War-Bereaved Families Association. It was conceived, not out of the growing awareness of Japan's war responsibilities, but as the government's response to a petition, submitted by the association organised by (not all) the families whose members were killed while serving the Japanese military. Long time recipients of the war pension, the members, as they reached old age, sought a construction of a memorial museum, to preserve in a tangible form, memories of their fathers.

The museum, like the *Enola Gay* exhibition, was planned for opening in 1995, the fiftieth anniversary of the end of the war. However, it was clear to anyone that any museum, especially if it was a national museum, could not memorialise the nation's past without a proper sense of critique. A series of advisory boards were summoned to discuss the character of the museum: all failed to reach agreement. The Japan War-Bereaved Families Association did not agree to any mention of Japan's wrongdoings. The final planning committee submitted three alternative proposals without recommending any: a display including Japanese aggressions; a display limited to the suffering of the Japanese; and a research library instead of a museum. The Japan War-Bereaved Families Association, however, was adamant about having a visual display.

To avoid all politically sensitive issues, the government's final decision focused on the display of the suffering that survivors had experienced, which would neither glorify nor accuse the dead. They chose not to display "materials that get into the discussion of the interpretation of our wartime history" (Yamaguchi 1996). On the first page of the exhibition catalogue, the museum states its mission objective:

[I]n recognition of the process in which Showa Hall has been planned as a memorial to the children of the military personnel who sacrificed their lives during the last war, the Ministry of Health and Welfare, as a part of the support it extends to war-bereaved families, proposes to convey to succeeding generations the daily hardships endured during and after the war by Japanese nationals and in particular by the children of the war dead and other members of war-bereaved families.

The goal of academics and concerned citizens who wished to build a national museum that would look squarely into the country's past and create a forum where history could be debated had been lost. All they could manage was to delay the opening till 1999.

Showa Hall and Its Topography

In the centre of Tokyo is what Roland Barthes calls "a sacred void," the Imperial Palace (Barthes 1982). On its eastern periphery lie public gardens famous for cherry blossoms. Located just outside the gardens, Showa Hall intimates a symbolic but not openly stated relationship with the Emperor. Further away from the palace, across the street from Showa Hall, stands Yasukuni Shrine, a controversial Shinto shrine dedicated to fallen Japanese soldiers. Because those enshrined include war criminals executed by the Tokyo War Criminal Tribunal, the shrine invites the furore of neighbouring Asian governments when it is officially visited by Japanese cabinet ministers. Scattered around the shrine are the statues of great generals and monuments dedicated to soldiers killed in action. The area surrounding the museum is suffused with memories of the war and exudes a sacred aura to veterans and their families. The majority of the museum visitors are groups of veterans and war-bereaved families who come to Yasukuni Shrine on their annual pilgrimage.

The silver coloured museum is eye-catching in its singularity of architectural style. I was told that the concept behind it was a store-house. Indeed it is a vault in which the memories of 3 million Japanese who died in the war are stored.[5] The hollow entrance to the museum suggests a *tori* (gate) placed at the entrance of a Shinto shrine. The gigantic *tori* of Yasukuni Shrine is merely a hundred meters away. Its shape also reminds me of ancient Japanese clay figurines (*dogu*)

---

[5]   On August 15, the day on which many Asian countries celebrate liberation from Japanese rule, in a huge arena near Showa Hall an annual ceremony to mourn the three million plus Japanese who died during the war is held with the Emperor in attendance. Broadcasted live on national television, shortly before noon the emperor offers his condolences, then the nation is asked to observe a minute of silence, though few actually do. What makes me uncomfortable is the repeated mention of the number three million plus throughout the service. It is becoming a symbolic number for the Japanese that ensures the total exclusion of some twenty million killed in Asia. The performative citation of the figure reiterated here and elsewhere portrays Japan as a victim, consecrates national history, and ultimately justifies the war.

typically of a pregnant woman depicted with her large belly and short legs spread out. Figuratively, the museum is both a womb and a tomb where soldiers, once taught to become children of the Emperor, are conceived and buried. They were told that once they died their souls would reunite at Yasukuni Shrine. During the war, the shrine's elaborately staged rites included the deification of those who died in the preceding year. In a torch-lit procession, priests carried a palanquin that was said to contain the spirits of the dead to the sanctuary. On this night, mothers lined the approach to the shrine to see their sons off.

The Showa Hall Display

The Showa Hall display replicates the mother-son relationship celebrated by Yasukuni Shrine. Upon entering the exhibition area, visitors are greeted by some forty *senninbari*, meaning literally one thousand stitches. During the war, mothers who sent their sons to the battlefield asked one thousand other women to each make a stitch on a rectangular cloth. Stitches were often made in the shape of a tiger, a brave and mythically auspicious animal, or in the shape of letters signifying victory. The time and effort it took them to complete such a cloth epitomised the affection of mothers for their sons. Soldiers wore them under their uniform as a talisman to protect them from enemy bullets. Directly across from the *senninbari*, letters that soldiers sent home are on display.

Claiming political neutrality, Showa Hall displays no panels that attempt to interpret history. No essays are printed in their catalogue. Gruesome photos that might horrify the visitors are nowhere to be found. *Senninbari* and the letters are about the only objects that evoke the presence of soldiers. On the wall leading to the next exhibition corner is an enlarged life-size photo of a flag-waving crowd, bidding farewell to departing soldiers at a train station. Upon scrutiny, however, one realises that soldiers are conspicuously absent from the photo. Showa Hall avoids with meticulous care any representations that might directly suggest the war. In its absence, emphasis is placed on the presence of home, the home front, and the mother.

The two floors of exhibition space are divided evenly between the periods of the war and its immediate aftermath. Going down the staircase, visitors are confronted with the front pages of newspapers from August 15, 1945, on which appears the Emperor's message announcing the end of the war. The imperial rescript begins with the famous appeal to Japanese subjects: "you have endured the unendurable…" the words rightly summing up the hardships that the people were forced to endure as the war approached its inevitable conclusion. The people's suffering included, among other things, conscripted labour, curtailed freedom of speech and movement, constant state surveillance, and the deaths of many loved ones. Yet Showa Hall displays none of those. It just transforms hardships into acceptable forms of representation.

The upper floor gallery includes exhibits that recall daily life during wartime, things such as ration tickets, wooden buckets used after everything that contained metal was "voluntarily turned in" to increase arms production, old school uniform, posters, medicine bottles and plastic replicas of the meagre food that was available at the time. But the display also includes items not related to war, everyday household objects such as a wooden ice box used before the days of the refrigerator, an old clock, a gramophone, and children's toys. Making a subtle connection with the *senninbari* display at the entrance, these items emphasise the mother's presence and memories of childhood. The display of hardships is thus turned into a discourse of home, personal origin and *nostalgia*.

Construction of Nostalgia

David Lowensthal states simply that "nostalgia is memory with the pain removed" (Lowensthal 1985: 8). Bryan Turner, in his more comprehensive review of the "nostalgic paradigm," cites "a departure from some golden age of 'homefulness'" (Turner 1987: 150) as one of his major components of nostalgia. Whether nostalgia deals with the past falsely, or accurately is not the point. It is more important to consider how nostalgia is used "in specially reconstructed ways" (Davis 1977: 417). Nostalgia is the feeling that I find powerfully evoked in Showa Hall. A newspaper article covering it's opening (*The Asahi Shimbun*, March 29, 1999: 38) summarises a characteristic reaction that the reporter observed among the first visitors to the museum: reminiscing of the days gone by. I have also overheard visitors speak fondly of the past on several occasions. At Showa Hall, the war has been transformed into something that the elderly can reminisce about.

Lighting and spatial arrangements help create a feeling of nostalgia. In a windowless, grotto-like intimacy, exhibits are placed on wooden shelves that impart warmth. Lighting is subdued. It is dark compared to the way other museum spaces are lit in Japan. The dim but warm glow of a remembered childhood permeates the space. The way Showa Hall creates a family atmosphere is characterised by James Clifford as the "boutique style" of display, which makes the exhibits seem not "out of place on the walls or coffee tables of middle class living rooms" (Clifford 1988: 228).

On video monitors, short clips from old newsreels are replayed over and over again. They feature such narratives as how school yards were turned to vegetable gardens to increase food production and how school children were evacuated to rural villages to escape strategic bombing of urban centres. Set to cheerful music, people in these films seem to be animated, even joyful. No explanations are offered. There is no mention of the fact that these were propaganda films designed to boost morale and conceal the reality of life.

Showa Hall allows visitors to regard the past with a retrospective gaze. Nostalgia presumes the innocence of remembering subjects. Reporting on how Westerners recollect their former colonial experiences, Renato Rosaldo observes, "nostalgia is a particularly appropriate emotion to invoke in attempting to establish one's innocence" (Rosaldo 1989: 108). Nostalgia is at once a selective memory and a selective amnesia that deals only with sweet remembrances. It consigns to oblivion shame, humiliation, and crimes that one has committed in the past.

Susan Stewart, in her analysis of memory in "On Longing," describes that "[n]ostalgia, like any form of narrative, is always ideological: the past it seeks has never existed except as narrative, and hence, always absent." (Stewart 1984: 23). Roland Robertson distinguishes two types of nostalgia. Following up Hobsbawm and Ranger's conceptualisation of "invention of tradition," Robertson associates what he calls "wilful nostalgia" with myth making strategies of emerging nation states toward the end of the nineteenth and in the early twentieth century. His inclusion of discussion of skilful "political exploitation of nostalgia" (Robertson 1990: 48) in Meiji Period Japan (1868-1912) is both appropriate and insightful. The political elites at that time dexterously instilled in the Japanese mind the notion of a racially and culturally homogeneous nation which had never existed before. Another type of nostalgia that Robertson mentions is contemporary "consumerist-simulational nostalgia" (Robertson 1990: 55) of the late capitalist global economy. Robertson, however, is careful to point out that the latter does not necessarily overwhelm the former, manifestly political "wilful nostalgia."

The point I wish to make is that nostalgia evoked by the mode of display at Showa Hall incorporates both of types that Robertson expounds on. Just as elderly visitors can reminisce about the past, a younger generation of visitors with no first hand memories of the war may be attracted to the sepia coloured exhibits that resemble kitsch simulation of the past commercially available everywhere outside the museum. But Showa Hall artfully frames the latter type of nostalgia

inside a nationalist narrative of the former. Its display conjures up an absent past that takes back visitors to their idealised origin, not only to their personal home, but also to a community identified as a nation.

Showa Hall assumes the position that hardships were suffered by all. And by doing so it purports to represent a collective memory of a people. Placed in a de-historicised and re-contextualised museum space, its display is metonymic. A collection of homely objects is made to stand for the experience of a whole nation. It attempts to objectify a national culture by the display of a single category of objects. It must be noted that only certain groups that have continued to constitute a majority and retain a dominant position in Japanese society share memories thus evoked. In Showa Hall, nowhere is mention made of "other" people such as comfort women, non-Japanese conscripted labourers, or imprisoned pacifists, just to name a few who suffered in ways much different from those mainstream Japanese whom the museum represents. Stuart Hall rightly points out that "identities can function as points of identification and attachment only because of their capacity to exclude, to leave out, to render 'outside'" (Hall 1996: 5).

The nostalgic narrative that Showa Hall constructs through its display is totalising and exclusive. It is also coupled with another narrative, that of national progress. If nostalgia is associated with a sense of loss that drives alienated moderns to seek solace in a lost origin of wholeness, the combination of the two narratives may strike one as strange. But in fact, the two are profoundly connected to each other. Instead of negating the present in favour of a lost origin, Showa Hall celebrates the post-war progress as a positive achievement. Its two narratives make clear that without the suffering shared in the past, present prosperity could not have been attained. It is the material comfort of today that allows visitors to look back on the past with nostalgia.

The way visitors perceive the objects on display is already narrativised when they enter the museum. Starting from the introductory corner of the *senninbari*, they are herded through a single corridor, unless one makes a determined effort to go back and forth along the route. The upper floor exhibition begins with the life at home in the 1930s, then proceeds with the shortage of food and materials, wartime school life, and ends with air raid drills. On the lower floor, themes are arranged in the order of post-war black markets, the lives of children, travail of mothers, and improving living standards. The finale of the exhibition is an affirmation of the post-war recovery and a promise of a brighter future. Here exhibits range from a motorcycle, the first post-war industrial product produced in Japan, to the first Nobel Prize awarded to a Japanese scientist. Moving visitors along the chronological axis traces a narrative of progress, conveying an unmistakable message that the wartime hardships have been deservedly rewarded.

Conclusion

History, when displayed publicly, can become a contentious site, especially when it purports to represent memories of a nation. Although Showa Hall feigns political neutrality, its metonymic mode of representation, which transforms the reality of war into nostalgic desire for a shared past, should, of necessity, be criticised.

The relationship between memory and history is problematic. We remember to forget, forget to remember. As Natalie Zemon Davis and Randolph Starn write, "forgetting is only the substitution of one memory for another" (Davis and Starn 1989: 2). We are constantly making a conscious and unconscious choice between what should remain within our memory and what should not. The case of Showa Hall illustrates how its display is intertwined with the process of constructing a publicly authenticated narrative history. By foregrounding hardships as a common experience of a people, Showa Hall translates traumatic experiences of war into the narratives of nostalgia and progress. In his well-known lecture delivered in 1882, Ernest Renan stressed the role that both shared memory and shared amnesia play in the construction of a nation. Suggesting how common suffering unites a people, he described a nation as "a large-scale solidarity, constituted by the feeling of the sacrifices that one has made in the past and of those that one is prepared to make in the future" (Renan 1990: 19). The ways in which Showa Hall organises its display echo the dominant political position that prescribes a unified and stable national identity. But the museum is silent on the point that the choice of such positionality is dependent on exclusion and abjection of others who are neither represented nor representable within it.

Works Cited

Althusser, L. "Ideology and Ideological State Apparatuses." *Lenin and Philosophy and Other Essays.* Trans., Ben Brewster. New York: Monthly Review Press, 1971.

Anderson, B. *Imagined Communities: Reflections on the Origin and Spread of Nationalism.* London: Verso, 1983.

Bauman, R. "American Folklore Studies and Social Transformation: A Performance-Centred Perspective." *Text and Performance Quarterly* 9 (1989): 175-184.

Barthes, R. *The Empire of Signs*. Trans. Richard Howard. New York: Hill and Wang, 1982.

Butler, J. "Performative Acts and Gender Constitution: An Essay in Phenomenology and Feminist Theory." *Performing Feminisms: Critical Theory and Theatre*, ed. Sue-Ellen Case. Baltimore and London: Johns Hopkins U. P., 1990a

Butler, J. *Gender Trouble: Feminism and the Subversion of Identity*. New York and London: Routledge, 1990b.

Clifford, J. *The Predicament of Culture: Twentieth-Century Ethnography, Literature, and Art.* Cambridge: Harvard U. P., 1988.

Clifford, J. *Routes: Travel and Translation in the Late Twentieth-Century.* Cambridge: Harvard U. P., 1997.

Conquergood, D. "Of Caravans and Carnivals: Performance Studies in Motion." *The Drama Review* 39.4 (1995): 137-141.

Dann, G. M. S. *The Language of Tourism: A Sociolinguistic perspective.* Wallingford: CAB International, 1996.

Davis, F. "Nostalgia, Identity, and the Current Nostalgia Wave." *Journal of Popular Culture* 11 (1977): 414-24.

Davis, N. Z. and Starn, R. "Introduction." *Representations* 26 (1989): 1-6.

Foucault, M. *Discipline and Punish: The Birth of the Prison.* London: Allen Lane, 1977.

Foucault, M. *Power/Knowledge: Selected Interviews and Other Writings, 1972-1977.* New York: Pantheon Books, 1980.

Hobsbawm, E. and Ranger T. eds. *The Invention of Tradition.* Cambridge: Cambridge U. P., 1983.

Hall, S. "Introduction: Who Needs Identity." *Questions of Cultural Identity*, eds. Stewart Hall and Paul du Gay. London: Sage, 1996. 1-17.

Karp, I. "Introduction." *Museums and Communities: The Politics of Public Culture*, eds. I. Karp, C. M. Kreamer, and S. D. Lavine. Washington and London: Smithsonian Institution Press, 1992. 1-17.

Karp, I. and Lavine, S. D. "Introduction: Museum and Multiculturalism." *Exhibiting Cultures: The Poetics and Politics of Museum Display*, eds. S.D. Lavine and I. Karp. Washington and London: Smithsonian Institution Press, 1991. 1-10.

Kirshenblatt-Gimblett, B. *Destination Culture: Tourism, Museums, and Heritage.* Berkeley: University of California Press. 1998.

Kohn, R. H. "History at Risk: The Cases of the *Enola Gay*." *History Wars: The Enola Gay and Other Battles for the American Past*, eds. E. T. Linenthal and T. Engelhardt. New York: Metropolitan Books, 1996. 140-70.

Kurin, R. *Reflections of a Culture Broker: A View from the Smithsonian.* Washington and London: Smithsonian Institution Press, 1997.

Lowenthal, D. *The Past is a Foreign Country.* Cambridge: Cambridge U. P., 1985

MacAloon, J. J. "Introduction: Cultural performances, Culture Theory." *Rite, Drama, Festival, Spectacle: Rehearsals Toward a Theory of Cultural Performance*, ed. John J. MacAloon. Philadelphia: Institute for the Study of Human Issues, 1984. 1-17.

Pratt, M. L. *Imperial Eyes: Travel Writing and Transculturation.* London: Routledge, 1992

Prince, G. *A Dictionary of Narratology.* Aldershot: Scholar Press, 1988.

Renan, E. "What is a Nation?" Trans. Martin Thom. *Nation and Narration*, ed. H. K. Bhabha. London: Routledge, 1990. 8-22.

Robertson, R. "After Nostalgia? Wilful Nostalgia and the Phases of Globalisation." *Theories of Modernity and Postmodernity*, ed. B. S. Turner. London: Sage, 1990.

Rosaldo, R. "Imperialist Nostalgia." *Representations* 26 (1989): 107-122.

Schechner, R. *Environmental Theater*. New York: Hawthorn Press, 1973.

Schechner, R. "Performance Studies: The Broad Spectrum Approach." *Phi Kappa Phi Journal*. Summer (1990): 15-16.

Schechner, R. "What is Performance Studies Anyway?" *The End of Performance*, eds. P. Phelan and J. Lane. New York: New York U. P., 1998. 357-362.

Schechner, R. unpublished manuscript. 2000.

Singer, M. *When a Great Tradition Modernises: An Anthropological Approach to Indian Civilisation*. Chicago: The University of Chicago Press, 1972.

Stewart, S. *On Longing: Narratives of the Miniature, the Gigantic, the Souvenir, the Collection*. Baltimore: The Johns Hopkins U. P., 1984.

Stone, A. "Hiroshima Display Ends in Rancour: Smithsonian Embroiled in Debate that Causes an 'Intellectual Bloodletting.'" *USA Today* February 1(1995): 1.

Turner, B. "A Note on Nostalgia." *Theory, Culture & Society* 4 (1987): 147-56.

Wallace, M. *Mickey Mouse History and Other Essays on American Memory*. Philadelphia: Temple U. P., 1997.

Yamaguchi, M. "Museum to Leave Out Dark Wartime Deeds." *Asahi Evening News* February 17 (1996): 3.

CHAPTER 9

The Journey to Con-Fusion:
Between Australia and Japan

NISHIDÔ Kôjin
translated by EGLINTON-SATÔ Mika

The Frame of Expression in the 1980s and 1990s

When I saw the collaborative performance by Gekidan Kaitaisha and NYID, the thought suddenly came to my mind – "this looks like the theatrical style of the 1990s." Of course, what I mean by 1990s style is not so simple and I do not intend to define the term simply in the context of Japan or Japanese performance. Rather, I intend to imply a kind of representational style that can be called "anti-1990s." In order to examine the 1990s style of expression, I have to start by establishing what the common characteristics and concepts were of the preceding decade, the 1980s.

When I think about 1980s styles of expression, the theatre of the Spanish company, La Fura dels Baus comes to mind. Their performance *Suz/O/Suz*, which was presented in Japan at the end of the 1980s, was their representative work. *Journey to Con-Fusion* clearly reminded me of La Fura's performance.

After the audience was led inside the warehouse performance space for *Suz/O/Suz* they realised that there was no seating or safe places to take refuge. The performance began in an atmosphere of brutality: the performers dragged oil-drums around and jumped into the audience while carrying chainsaws; they threw fresh meat and flour everywhere and the smell of animals' blood mixed with wine filled the space. This series of actions was controlled to some extent and of course did not simply aim to promote raw violence. Nevertheless this physical act still conveyed a strong sensation of brutality. It would not be a mis-interpretation to read into these actions the fighting instinct that is often celebrated among Spanish people. Meanwhile, the audience was frantically running left and right, which by contrast seemed to hint at the Asian mentality of avoiding physical contact.

In my opinion, 1980s-style expression is a performance style similar to that of the 1960s and 1970s in terms of physicality, yet slightly different in terms of its radicalism. In the case of the 1980s, a critical consciousness was evident, which departs from the optimistic 1960s tendency towards the happy unity of the audience and performer. This feeling of unity was linked to the community-oriented movement of the 1960s that was replaced in the 1980s by a harder edge.

Even though the beginning of *Journey to Con-Fusion* shared similarities with that of La Fura – the audience entered an open space without seating – the main body of the performance developed differently. By considering this difference, I think it may be possible to define the position of 1990s theatre as divergent from both the typical 1980s style and that of the 1960s and 1970s. The theatre of the 1990s intended to *subvert* both the theatre of the 1960s and the theatre of the 1980s. That is, by comparing these two paradigms of theatre, I am able to grasp the paradigm of 1990s theatre.

Fusion and/or Rapture with the Audience?

Let's examine the performance *Journey to Con-Fusion* chronologically. When I took off my shoes and entered the Morishita Studio, I found the audience were all standing around. Soon two performers came to me and started to interview me. One was Australian and the other was Japanese. (A video camera followed them around and live images of the interviews were transmitted to large projection screens installed at each end of the space.) The Australian actor began with her self-introduction in Japanese and then asked the following questions in English: "What is your favourite sport?" "Do you believe in life after death?" My answer to the first question was "Of course, it's football," and the second "No, I don't." To my unenthusiastic attitude, she said "thanks" in faltering Japanese and moved on.

Later I found that other performers had been reciting messages into other microphones such as "The Sydney Olympics does not exist" and "Sport is fascism." In short, they were making a protest against the politics associated with the Olympics movement and specifically the Sydney Olympics that were due to take place later that year. In this context my answers were far off the mark; I even thought that I had no right to take part in the performance.

After this opening sequence, the main body of the performance began. Each performer started walking around the space, seemingly at random, until gradually they all took the same path through the audience. Then the individual performers merged into one walking group. The strictly controlled manner of the walking body – or mass – seemed to represent a single will.

Some slides were projected onto the white projection screens. At the same time a spotlight started to outline a performance space in the centre of the room. The audience naturally avoided this and sat around it.

As the audience sat there with anticipation, I noticed that they were not sitting forwards but leaning backwards. In spite of the free space, an invisible line or border emerged between the "performance space" (as I will temporarily call it) and the "audience space." This situation bewildered me. Does this performance intend to "infuse" the performers and the audience, or "separate" one from the other, I wondered?

On the screen, one actor's personal history was being narrated, in the style of a "confession." Looking at it, I felt unengaged.

What struck me was the question of why did David Pledger (the director of this scene) choose this space? How did he understand the sense of fusion and rapture between performer and audience? If he intended to make a border between the two, why did he not address this point in advance? Before I managed to grasp his intentions, the performance moved onto the next scene. Not being answered, these questions remained with me.

Bodies of the Diaspora

As the performance evolved, Kaitaisha's regular movements were recognisable.

My attention was drawn to one set of actions in particular. Japanese and Australian performers were doing the same gestures and movements. I wonder whether it is possible to call it "dance"? For me, it seemed like a monkey dance; loose bodies were just moving without intentions. This scene emphasised the differences of physicality between the bodies of the Japanese and Australian performers. Alternatively, it represented two differing bodies in one action. The Kaitaisha performers seemed awfully oppressed and distorted. In contrast, the Australians', with their erect spines, seemed more articulated and healthy.

Seeing this difference gave rise to a number of thoughts. Human existence is always perceived as something physical. However, after enduring extreme labour, or inhuman experiences such as torture, the human body can be reduced to something like a rag doll. When people are deprived of adequate living conditions they lose their cultural trappings and human dignity. They are reduced to the level of being "mere bodies" equal to all other material things.

The physicality of Kaitaisha belongs to this dimension, where emaciated and deprived bodies are being produced. In Kaitaisha's performance, the body is associated with the idea of diaspora and is ranked below the healthy bodies that might symbolise the forces of coercion and exploitation.

In this regard Kaitaisha's representation of the body is a strong and marked contrast to the corporeality of typical 1980s theatre. As I have already suggested, the bodies of La Fura dels Baus are like those of colonisers and cannibals. They use their bodies to make the audience feel uneasy. But in order to break down the distance between the audience and performer, one more step is needed: a step in the direction of "strong wills," which the audience would be able to feel and recognise through the bodies of NYID performers. For the performers of Kaitaisha, however, who expose the existence of deprived and useless bodies, those "strong wills" are unattainable. Metaphorically speaking, in a European context, performing bodies that can "express" something are bodies that can step forward and progress; this is to rise up from the self-conscious and one's inner world. Yet there still exists the body that Kaitaisha tries to enact, the body that has no choice but to accept the status quo and is ultimately to be always rendered "passive."

The performance of bodies in Kaitaisha reminds me of Grotowski's theory of the theatre – which is also a theory of the body. It is clear that his theory is nearer to "the bodies of diaspora" model and the antithesis of the elite strong willed body. In terms of comparative theatre, the difference between the East and the West is this "passive" body – that can be seen at the core of Eastern theatre developments, including Grotowski in Eastern Europe (while the opposite developed in the West).

The Deprived Body

It may be said that the idea of the "passive body" came to the forefront of theatre in the 1990s. Theatrical activities started to focus on neglected themes; such notions as "cool desire" and "the emaciated body." These themes appeared on the stage as a new type of expression. But I want to question this point a little further – how can Japanese artists express ideas of diaspora? In the Asian context, Japan is obviously a dominant power and on the side of the forces of exploitation. Even though Kaitaisha aligns with the deprived in Japanese society, one cannot simply refer to them as "diaspora-like." It is necessary to keep in mind the fact that the condition of "the deprived body" that is expressed in Kaitaisha's work lives within the society of the exploiter.

This point leads us to complicated issues about the contemporary status of the nation state. Shimizu points out that the political struggles of the 1990s grew from the emergence of so-called "North-South" conflicts. These developed following the end of the Cold War; a conflict described as being between "East" and "West." Judging by Japanese economic power, Japan belongs to the "Northern" world. But that does not always mean that Japanese theatre groups and artists belong in the same category as other more powerful institutions. For example, in this production Shimizu asked his Japanese performers to perform semi-naked. In comparison, Pledger naturally clothed his Australian performers. This moment points to important differences between the companies. Shimizu regarded the Japanese bodies as the bodies of cattle. In comparison, Pledger had one performer verbalise his/her story in the style of a confession or history. This suggested that he tried to establish a sense of meaning using words as a cultural phenomenon. From these differences, Kaitaisha's position as "Southern" became clear. Shimizu means to expose his performers' bodies in the way of the "South."

But this is by no means straightforward. There are twists to the logic of representation here because Kaitaisha's "bodies of the South" are also in a sense fictional. They are clearly not the same as the bodies of homeless people who wander around cities. How can you portray a body that you really do not know? Is it even possible to represent such "deprived bodies" to begin with? As a way of resolving these doubts, Kaitaisha has chosen to torture their bodies to the limit (of actual damage). One example of this is when one performer repeatedly slaps another on their back making the skin turn red. Another example is found in a sequence performed between a male and female performer; as she keeps jumping away from him, he catches her. This simple repetition has a wearing effect on one's thoughts. When you are pushed into an extreme situation, you will be forced to stop thinking and become like an automatic machine. The process to reach this "suspension of judgment" has become part of Kaitaisha's artistic expression. Violence is the medium through which they work. Shimizu aims to focus on the question of how to reveal bodies "without intention" in performance. So far there is no established method to express such a condition, the performers' bodies just wait for the time after which the "unready" body is revealed by accident. In order to create that chance, the company must give up any desires or purpose; they must remove the aim to express intention.

The Necessity of the Collaboration

Bodies conditioned by the "South" are just like the materialistic bodies that appear in times of crisis. These bodies never try to accuse somebody or question through their existence. This is because "accusation" is a dramaturgy that is liable to forge a structure where the maimed bodies (of the "South") are "accusing" the sound bodies (of the "North"). In that kind of structure, "the bodies of the South" can take the moral ground and are in a superior position. However, this is a reversal – a perversion – that is acceptable only in the art world, it is not a true indication of the status quo. On the contrary this "superiority" experienced in the art world becomes *inferiority* in the real world, because the "North" is still exploiting the "South." In this way, the power of art – while seemingly sensitive to the under-class – in fact covers-up the harsh reality (of North-South relations).

In this situation, it is important to realise that artistic forms are unable to define or impose their own value on the world. If you follow this rule, the body can stand for all forms of expression. Thus, I resist the idea that the artists' intention is self-evident and privileged. I believe that artists come into being for a limited time and in particular contexts. The performer needs a certain consensus with the audience (in order to perform). Only when the audience and the performer stand in an equal position sharing one stage can the performers reveal themselves as they are, and not as a substitute for somebody else. If this is the case, it follows that there is no directed stage event with values that have been decided in advance, but it is the audience that discovers the value of the performance on the spot. To arrive at this situation, two "bodies" (i.e. the audience and the performers) should stand equal. Then finally we may consider the performance of bodies that might transcend matters of affirmation and negation. This will lead us to indeterminable values being seen on the stage.

I think the ultimate object of the collaboration can be found in these indeterminable values. In working together, the two groups have discovered so many differences; these will become powerful resources for creation in the future. Is it necessary to have collaborations? Through their differences, what can the two groups create? If the border between them is to open and a "hybrid" state emerges, then the two must share a common feeling: "we are both being deprived." The "Journey to Con-Fusion" has just begun.

CHAPTER 10

Journey to Con-Fusion:
Photo Essay

Miyauchi Katsu

Members of Gekidan Kaitaisha and NYID in *Journey to Con-Fusion*
(Open Stage, University of Melbourne, 1999)

Katia Molino, Greg Ulfan, Aota Reiko, *Journey to Con-Fusion* (1999)

Journey to Con-Fusion 2 (Morishita Studio, Tokyo 2000)

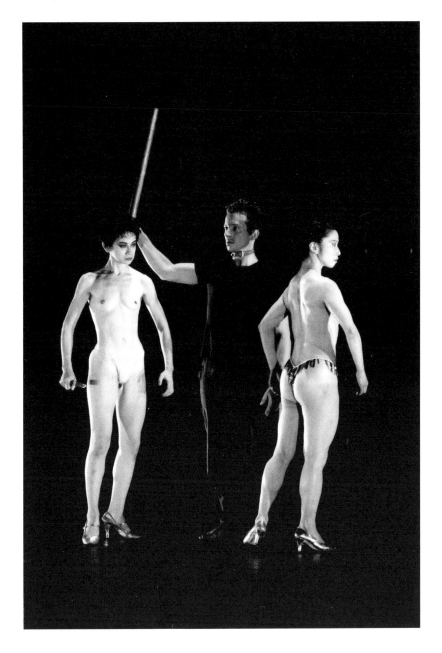

Nakajima Miyuki, Simon Kingsley, Hino Hiruko,
Journey to Con-Fusion (1999)

Journey to Con-Fusion (1999)

Journey to Con-Fusion workshop (1999)

Journey to Con-Fusion workshop (1999)

Journey to Con-Fusion (1999)

154

Journey to Con-Fusion workshop (1999)

NYID Director David Pedger and performers, *Journey to Con-Fusion* workshop (1999)

Translator Yumi Umiumare, Kaitaisha Director Shimizu Shinjin, NYID Director
David Pedger and performers, *Journey to Con-Fusion* workshop (1999)

Journey to Con-Fusion 2 workshop (2000)

Journey to Con-Fusion 2 workshop (2000)

Journey to Con-Fusion 2 (2000)

Journey to Con-Fusion 2 (2000)

Journey to Con-Fusion 2 (2000)

Journey to Con-Fusion 2 (2000)

Journey to Con-Fusion 2 workshop (2000)

Journey to Con-Fusion 2 workshop (2000)

Journey to Con-Fusion 2 workshop (2000)

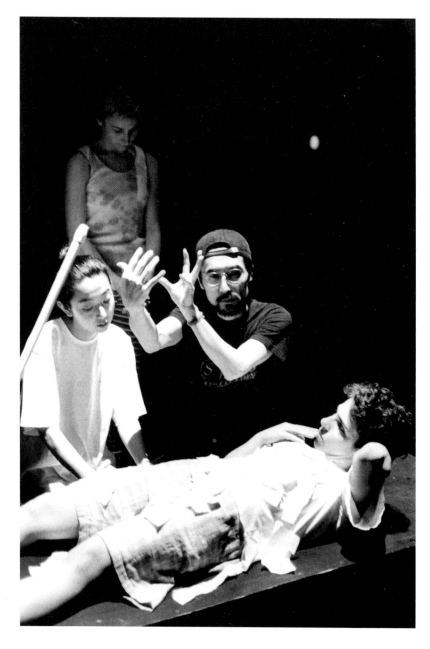

Translator Inoue Ai, Kaitaisha Director Shimizu Shinjin, Katia Molino,
Journey to Con-Fusion 2 workshop (2000)

Journey to Con-Fusion 2 (2000)

After 9.11

UCHINO Tadashi

We are living now in the post-9.11 space. Whatever this means, we should all assume that any critical thought must start from thinking about what this can and should mean. It is well known that Adorno said that "after Auschwitz, it is barbaric to write poetry," and we must at least start from the question of whether or not it is barbaric to write poetry after 9.11. 9.11 and the ensuing developments have exposed us to vast amounts of information (including manipulation of information) and interpretations which we cannot possibly fully process. But what we ought take into account is the viewpoint, recently and concisely expressed by Derrida at one of his lectures, which can be found on Akira Asada's *Hihyô Kukan* (Critical Space) website.

> I have absolute sympathy for the victims of 9.11, but nevertheless I must say that, in this crime, not a single person is innocent in a political sense. And if my sympathy for all the innocent victims is infinite, it also means that my sympathy is not limited to the victims who died in 9.11. This in fact is my interpretation of what it is that has since yesterday been called "infinite justice," according to the White House slogan. One should not excuse one's mistakes and errors in policy even at the very moment of paying that horrendous price, which may be inconceivably unfair. (Secondary translation from Akira Asada's Japanese translation, see also Akira 2000)

Even if we have to admit this is very delicate phrasing, the assumption we must take into account is this: although it should be obvious that no one is innocent "in a political sense" "in this crime," this awareness does not seem to be the case, at least at the level of Japan's mass media and their perception of reality. "Not a single person is innocent in a political sense;" whether it be the numerous victims considered to be "innocent," whether one is for or against the American economic hegemony, or whether one says or not (building on Hardt and Negri's concept of "Empire," 2000), that it is because no one can be outside "Empire." That we could not have prevented this act of terrorism, or that we could not have prevented the ensuing retaliatory attacks, or that we cannot stop massacres in Palestine at this point, does not imply that "not a single person is innocent in a political sense."

But here I am not attempting to launch a call to join in the anti-movements, nor am I professing "sinking into cynicism," saying that we ought to follow our conscience and remain quiet since nothing can be done anyway. What I am saying is that we must start from doing what, after 9.11, has become clear we ought to do.

So what is it that we ought to do? As Otori Hidenaga says, it can be nothing else but that "all of us – writers, critics, and researchers alike – must respond to the situation where Empire has come to cover the entirety of our communal territory" and not "excuse ourselves." (Otori 2002: 182). In spite of the fact that Derrida made the aforementioned lecture soon after the attack, it was in this context that he entitled it "The Language of the Other." And after 9.11, even I – who has neither that kind of competence, nor that kind of knowledge – am endeavouring, as a theatre critic, to write theatre reviews with the consciousness that the agenda we need to grapple with has clearly changed.

***

In the first issue of *Performing Arts*, a magazine published by Kyoto University of Arts and Design in May 2002, I wrote the above, somewhat melodramatic response to 9.11, in order to reason with myself for the need to keep writing. I say "melodramatic," in the sense that when I come back to my senses after a while, so to speak, I realise that this passage is only a reaffirmation of a project that I, along with others, had already started participating in, namely, an intra-cultural journey of critical thought that many of us in an age of globalisation have began.

"Intra-cultural" not "inter-cultural," because if an age of globalisation is an age of "Empire" in Hardt and Negri's sense, there is no in-between space or clearly demarcated boundaries, but an all-encompassing intra-ness, to whatever cultural practice we are engaged in. Thus, I would rather like to use the word globality rather than globalisation, as globalisation seems to refer to a pre-existing telos, where its process is supposed to have an end. Globality is the reality we should find ourselves entrapped in, not in the process of globalisation; in its sheer totality, as in "Empire," there is no exit, or no alternative space. All we can hope for is to briefly establish an ephemeral and temporary space of alternatives, and make a performative record out of this, before being forced to be erased and sent into oblivion. We should move fast enough so that there will be tons of different kinds of written records of such intra-cultural critical thoughts, before being co-opted and appropriated into the fixed territories of "academia," "journalism," and so on.

This volume is exactly the written record of the beginning of such an intra-cultural journey of critical thought in the context of the total dominance of globality. Here is a collection of essays of an unusual combination, of a gathering between cultural producers living in Japan and Australia. Most of them were at first presented at a conference in Tokyo a few years ago. It was indeed an exciting moment of emergence of trans-local sites of thinking and debating. There was almost no "we," essentialised subject positions, except in the sense that all participants temporarily fabricated a performing "we" during and only during the conference. The precious memory persists, but without this published record, the memory only serves as nostalgia. I thank Peter Eckersall and Moriyama Naoto for making my nostalgia an accessible history. Without them, the occasion was only to remain in participants' mind and nowhere else.

Works Cited

Akira, Asada. "Adorno, Derrida," *Nami*, February (2002).
Otori, Hidenaga. "Images of 'Empire," *Eureka*, March (2002).
Hardt, Michael. & Negri, Antonio. *Empire.* Cambridge, Mass.: Harvard U. P., 2000.

Contributors

Peter Eckersall is Senior Lecturer in Theatre Studies at the University of Melbourne and dramaturg for NYID.

Rachel Fensham is Senior Lecturer in Theatre and Performance Studies at Monash University.

Kitano Keisuke is Associate Professor of Culture and Communications at Niigata University.

Miyauchi Katsu is a photographer who specialises in theatre documentation.

Moriyama Naoto is Lecturer in Theatre Studies at the Kyoto University of Fine Arts and Design.

Nishidô Kôjin is a theatre critic and Associate Professor of Theatre Studies at Kinki University.

Katherine Mezur is a researcher in theatre and dance at the University of California at Santa Barbara.

Edward Scheer is Senior Lecturer in Theatre and Performance Studies at the University of New South Wales.

Takahashi Yuichiro is Professor of Performance Studies at Dokkyo University.

Uchino Tadashi is Associate Professor of Theatre Studies at the University of Tokyo.

Denise Varney is Senior Lecturer in Theatre Studies at the University of Melbourne.

Project Acknowledgements

Journey to Con-Fusion
8-13 December 1999. The Open Stage, University of Melbourne.
Artistic Directors: David Pledger and Shimizu Shinjin.
Performers: Kaitaisha – Hino Hiruko, Kumamoto Kenjiro, Nakajima
Miyuki, Moriyama Masako, Nomoto Ryoko, Urasoe Hisafumi, Aota Reiko,
Tsuchimoto Tadashi, Urayama Mariko, Akaiwa Kazumi, Fujishiro Aki,
Hasegawa Tomoko. NYID – Katia Molino, Greg Ulfan, Paul Bongiovanni,
Louise Taube, Simon Kingsley.
Translator: Yumi Umiumare.
Dramaturg: Peter Eckersall.
Producers: Hata Takeshi and Peter Eckersall.

Journey to Con-Fusion 2
1-9 July 2000. Morishita Studio, Tokyo.
Artistic Directors: Shimizu Shinjin and David Pledger.
Performers: NYID – Katia Molino, Greg Ulfan, Louise Taube, Simon
Kingsley. Kaitaisha – Hino Hiruko, Kumamoto Kenjiro, Nakajima Miyuki,
Nomoto Ryoko, Urasoe Hisafumi, Aota Reiko, Tsuchimoto Tadashi,
Urayama Mariko, Akaiwa Kazumi, Fujishiro Aki, Hasegawa Tomoko, Ishii
Yasuji.
Translator: Inoue Ai.
Dramaturg: Peter Eckersall.
Producers: Hata Takeshi and Peter Eckersall.

Journey to Con-Fusion 3
April-May 2002. The Open Stage & Dancehouse, Next Wave Festival,
Melbourne.
Artistic Directors: David Pledger and Shimizu Shinjin.
Performers: Kaitaisha – Hino Hiruko, Kumamoto Kenjiro, Nakajima
Miyuki, Urasoe Hisafumi, Aota Reiko, Adam Broinowski. NYID – Greg
Ulfan, Louise Taube, Simon Kingsley, Natalie Cursio.
Translator: Yumi Umiumare.
Dramaturg & Production manager: Peter Eckersall.
Producer: David Pledger.
Kaitaisha Company, Production and Tour Manager: Hata Takeshi.
Technical Manager and Lighting Designer: Paul Jackson.
Stage Manager: Angela Hicks.

Dramaturgies

Texts, Cultures and Performances

This series presents innovative research work in the field of twentieth-Century dramaturgy, primarily in the anglophone and francophone worlds. Its main purpose is to re-assess the complex relationship between textual studies, cultural and/or performance aspects at the dawn of this new multicultural millennium. The series offers discussions of the link between drama and multiculturalism (studies of minority playwrights – ethnic, aboriginal, gay and lesbian), reconsiderations of established playwrights in the light of contemporary critical theories, studies of the interface between theatre practice and textual analysis, studies of marginalized theatrical practices (circus, vaudeville etc.), explorations of the emerging postcolonial drama, research into new modes of dramatic expressions and comparative or theoretical drama studies.

The Series Editor, **Marc MAUFORT**, is Professor of English literature and drama at the *Université Libre de Bruxelles*.

Series Titles

No.12– Malgorzata BARTULA & Stefan SCHROER, *On Improvisation. Nine Conversations with Roberto Ciulli*, 2003, ISBN 90-5201-185-0

No.11– Peter ECKERSALL, UCHINO Tadashi & MORIYAMA Naoto (eds.), *Alternatives. Debating Theatre Culture in the Age of Con-Fusion*, 2004, ISBN 90-5201-175-3

No.10– Rob BAUM, *Female Absence. Women, Theatre, and Other Metaphors*, 2003, ISBN 90-5201-172-9

No.9– Marc MAUFORT, *Transgressive Itineraries. Postcolonial Hybridizations of Dramatic Realism*, 2003, ISBN 90-5201-990-8

No.8– Ric KNOWLES, *Shakespeare and Canada: Essays on Production, Translation, and Adaptation*, 2004, ISBN 90-5201-989-4

No.7– Barbara OZIEBLO & Miriam LÓPEZ-RODRIGUEZ, *Staging a Cultural Paradigm. The Political and the Personal in American Drama*, 2002, ISBN 90-5201-990-8

No.6– Michael MANHEIM, *Vital Contradictions. Characterization in the Plays of Ibsen, Strindberg, Chekhov and O'Neill*, 2002, ISBN 90-5201-991-6

No.5– Bruce BARTON, *Changing Frames. Medium Matters in Selected Plays and Films of David Mamet* (provisional title) (forthcoming), ISBN 90-5201-988-6

No.4– Marc MAUFORT & Franca BELLARSI (eds.), *Crucible of Cultures. Anglophone Drama at the Dawn of a New Millennium*, 2002 (second printing 2003), ISBN 90-5201-982-7

No.3– Rupendra GUHA MAJUMDAR, *Central Man. The Paradox of Heroism in Modern American Drama*, 2003, ISBN 90-5201-978-9

No.2– Helena GREHAN, *Mapping Cultural Identity in Contemporary Australian Performance*, 2001, ISBN 90-5201-947-9

No.1– Marc MAUFORT & Franca BELLARSI (eds.), *Siting the Other. Re-visions of Marginality in Australian and English-Canadian Drama*, 2001, ISBN 90-5201-934-7

Peter Lang—The website

Discover the general website of the Peter Lang publishing group:

www.peterlang.net

You will find

– an online bookshop of currently about 21,000 titles from the entire
  publishing group, which allows quick and easy ordering
– all books published since 1992
– an overview of our journals and series
– contact forms for new authors and customers
– information about the activities of each publishing house

Come and browse! We look forward to your visit!